DJ Charpentier

For Pat,
And this one's special for Mom & Dad

Other Books by DJ Charpentier

Fiction
Reggie Slater Mystery Series

Bethany Blues
Ocean City Blues
Key West Blues
Return to Bethany Beach

Russ Deever Mystery Series
Beach Blues
Carousel Blues
Marginal Blues

Nonfiction
As Luck Would Have It...Changing Your Mind:
A Practical Guide to Retirement
First Edition and Second Edition
As Luck Would Have It...*5-Years Later*
Retire Well!

All titles are available for Kindle or in print at Amazon.com

Table of Contents

"The basis of democracy is the willingness to assume well about other people."

Marilynn Robinson

"As I grow older, I pay less attention to what men say. I just watch what they do."

Andrew Carnegie

Preface

Most people that I know are honest or at least they try to be. Those folks are also doing what they believe to be the best that they can. This writing explores those sorts of people that believe in this type of ethical behavior and in contrast; those that do not.

The honest, good-hearted souls among us tend to believe that those who are dishonest get their comeuppance in the end; thus their belief in heaven and hell. We all know that that this is not what really happens all the time. Those who believe themselves to be privileged, usually are and can complicate the lives of honest people to their own gain. Honest people wish this was not so, but sadly it is.

We need our law enforcement and our judicial system to step up to the plate and act as the system of balance that they are meant to be. When those we trust put on a uniform or the robe, it signifies that they are now in a position that we revere and hold as special. They are not the people they are everyday, but the judges and police that protect the rights of all against the evils in the world.

This novel calls for those meant to keep the balance of power to sit up and take notice. To see the wrong and right it; to recognize evil and punish it; to hold the scales of legal balance steady so that they do not favor the few or the privileged.

D J Charpentier

Chapter 1: Down on the Corner

"Mornin', Punk."

"Mornin', Ed," Punk replied as the day began in the small city dominated by textile mills. There were few clouds and the day held the promise of more sweltering heat. The working men had already made their way to the several textile factories in the area filling the streets with workers carrying lunch pails: meeting their colleagues for another day of labor in the noisy, stuffy, and dusty factories. The last week had been brutal in the manufacturing town amongst the mills and three-decker tenements where little breeze brought minimal relief from the heavy, moist air.

"Where is everyone?" asked Ed to no one in particular as they sat on the curb next to the filling station.

"Just bein' lazy I guess." It was the middle of the summer and no young teenage boy has a reason to roll out of bed early. No school, too young for a job...why get up?

"We've got to get busy with something," said Ed. "We need to get out of this heat somehow."

" You're right about that, but what?" asked Punk. "Ed, its 1937 and we got no car and no money. We're stuck in this little city with no pool and no beach. The fire department won't even crack a hydrant because of the water shortage. Again...what?"

"Punk, you sometimes have no imagination. Here come the rest of the guys now. We just have to think."

Ed, Punk, and the rest of the neighborhood boys met and hung out each day at the filling station. Sometimes they would help out around the place, but most times they just passed the day waiting to get older to join their fathers in the mills.

"So, Al, what do you think? What can we do to get out of this heat?" Al, skinny as a rail, with bony fingers and arms looked around the group.

"Heck, I don't know. I'm only glad I had breakfast this morning and my father dragged his drunk-ass home last night. It was rather peaceful that he went right to bed instead of riling my mother and starting a fight. I'm good thanks."

"I've got something," said Omer. "Why don't we go down to Cohassett Beach, swim in the bay, and meet some girls?"

"Why not indeed," said Alfred. "Got a couple of reasons...no job...no money...no ride."

"That's three, dummy," nudged Punk who didn't outweigh Al, but by a few pounds.

"He's just learning," added Al. "But he has a point...or at least three points."

"Omer's idea is good, but we really only lack one thing that might get us all the rest," summarized Ed.

"Money!" They all answered.

"And how do we get it...no job, remember," said Alfred kicking at the dirt.

"Collect...it's all we got. It's the middle of the week and everyone has bottles they have not returned. We can collect them like we have done before. Check the empty lots and parking lots, outside the liquor stores, maybe even a few at our houses. Then, if we put it all together and return them to the grocery store, we got money...so, we got a ride on the trolley...and, we can get to Cohassett Beach. We work today, but we play tomorrow." After Ed's speech they were all off searching for bottle returns for the day. They scoured their own homes and the neighborhood lots for discarded bottles.

By the end of the day they had enough money for the trolley fare and some leftover for food and fun at the beach. The next day would be a day to remember.

+++++++

The air was still in the mill town as the boys gathered for their adventure the following morning. The machinery could be heard clanging and buzzing from the three-story red brick factories that surrounded the housing areas. You could almost see the heat reflecting off the brick and heating up the tenement houses, the small yards, and the narrow streets.

The group made their way down to the trolley station and boarded the Providence line. The route would take them through the Pawtucket mill area, down North Main Street, and into the City of Providence. There they boarded the Warwick trolley which would continue southward with stops in Edgewood, Lakewood, Hoxie, Conimicut, and on to Cohassett Beach Boulevard. The Boulevard was a wide divided affair with lanes for both cars and trolleys. They saw few cars and only encountered one trolley moving in the opposite direction.

Nearing Cohassett Beach, Alfred pointed to the tower of the roller coaster and other amusements creating the Cohassett Beach skyline in the distance. The amusement area was eerily silent this early in the day as they came into the station. The boys disembarked the trolley at the Cohassett station and made their way through the amusement midway.

As they walked toward the beach, the boys first passed the carousel at the top of the hill with its multicolored ponies and giant glass doors now open to the bright sunny day. Music from the band boxes punctuated the air as they passed; gazing in at the mirrored glass revolving as the ponies rose and fell in their circular flight. Mechanics could be seen greasing and oiling the mechanisms of the amusement ride.

From the sidewalk at the top of the hill by the carousel, they could see down past the arcade, the restaurants, and the midway, all the way down to the beach.

"Let's get cool before we do anything else," suggested Omer. They all agreed and quickly made their way down the sticky sidewalk to the beach. Once there, they shed their clothes and wearing bathing suits they had underneath, plunged into the cooling salt waters of East Greenwich Bay. The water cleansed the sweat from their bodies and revitalized their souls from the caldron that they faced daily in the sweltering city. This was the life...and they splashed and swam until they were tired. At last they lay on the beach napping in the sun.

"Wow, that felt good," Alfred softly said to no one in particular.

"You, bet," other voices echoed.

"I could do this every day," remarked Ed.

"We all could, but remember..."

Several voices answered..." No job, no car, no money." And they all laughed.

"It won't always be that way," said Al. "Soon we'll be old enough to get work. Then we'll have money...maybe even a car."

"Yeah," said Omer, "But then we'll we have no time?" and several of the boys threw articles of clothing at him.

Around noon, using their pooled money, they bought and shared some clam cakes, doughboys, and soda for lunch. They were like kings that owned the world as they sat along the seawall, facing the bay with the sea breeze in their faces, and enjoyed the feast.

"You boys look like you're having quite a day." The boys turned to look at the stranger that had spoken behind them. He was maybe in his early twenties, tall and slender, with the makings of a thin moustache along his upper lip. He was impeccably dressed in two-toned shoes, creased pants, a shirt open at the throat, and a vest. He had a matching jacket slung casually over his shoulder. The girl he was with was a looker. She wore a fitted red dress with a frilled hem, matching pumps, and a pill hat. She was displaying plenty of calf and cleavage for the entire world to see.

"We're on a bit of a holiday from the city," answered Omer. "We pooled our money, took the trolley, and came to the beach for the day."

"Sounds like a great plan. My name is Obie. Glad to meet you," he said shaking hands, "And this is my wife, Fritch. Say hello, honey."

"Hi, boys." She said and the boys all tripped over their tongues trying to reply with a coherent remark.

"We are renting a house here in the beach just a block from here. Would you like to come by later in the afternoon for some refreshment before you go back?" Obie offered.

The boys agreed and Obie gave them directions. They watched as Obie and Fritch sashayed up the avenue.

"Hochie mama! Did you get a load of that?"

"Put your tongue back into your mouth, Al. She's spoken for," said Ed playfully slapping Al in the back of the head. "Let's have some fun at the arcade with the spare money we have and then stop by their rental. That would be about right to catch the trolley back in time for supper."

The boys went up the avenue away from the beach and spent an hour in the penny arcade. They played shooting games, pinball, and ski-ball. They amassed enough prize tickets to get two free-ride tickets each.

They didn't have to spend too much money on the pinball because Al was so good, he kept getting free games for them all. The group played their fill and moved to the carousel. They all chose outside horses of course and readied themselves for the ride to start. As the ride increased its circular motion a man climbed the stairs and put the rings loudly into the hopper. He swung the arm out so the outer riders could reach for a ring.

As riders passed, they hung out from their horse and snatched a ring from the end of the arm. The prize, a free ride, was represented by a brass ring. Most of the rings were silver. Silver rings were tossed toward a target of a clown's mouth as the riders passed.

Suddenly, there was a cry of "I got it." It was Ed holding the brass ring high above his head swinging it on his finger. The boys all patted him on the back when the ride was over. They had enough free tickets left for one ride each and the one free pass for the carousel.

The boys noticed there was a young boy about six years old crying on the sidelines pointing at the carousel. He wanted a ride, but his parents were trying to explain that they could not afford it. Ed looked at the group and they all nodded. Ed walked over to the boy and gave him the free pass. As they left the carousel building, they could see the young boy with his Dad holding him on one of the large horses moving up and down, whizzing around, and beaming from ear to ear.

The group decided that the Dodgem Cars were it for the last ride. The large building stood across the street from the Carousel with the word Dodgem painted in big black letters across the façade.

The cars of the Dodgem ran on a metal floor and had a pole with a spring connector rising to the ceiling. The cars were inert until the ride operator energized the circuit and electricity flowed to the motors propelling the cars. The cars' speed was controlled by a floor pedal. Each car had a large wheel that controlled its direction.

The boys all got on the same ride with a few other patrons and sped around the course lining each other up for a head-on and sometimes two ganging up on one for a sideward jolt. The cars sparked and bumped until the ride operator hit the off switch and the cars glided to a halt. They all exited the ride breathless and recounting their best hits still taunting each other with boasts of the best surprise crashes from behind.

The cottage rented by Obie and Fritch, if you could call it that, amounted to a bedroom and small, eat-in kitchen. When the boys arrived, there was a pot of steamed clams coming off the stove and generous bowls were served to all. The steamers had been plucked from the nearby cove just that afternoon. The couple was ecstatic to be at "the beach" for a week and swore they would always return for their vacation.

About three in the afternoon the boys said their 'thank-yous' and 'goodbyes.' They had eaten their fill and thoroughly enjoyed the company of Obie and Fritch. Catching the trolley at the Cohassett Beach station, they made their way across the wooden bridge to Buttonwoods leaving the carnival midway behind. The trolley then made a turn northward and back toward Providence and the mill towns leaving the coolness of the beach behind. It was a day they would all remember.

Chapter 2: Return to Me

"Hand me that three-eighths." Punk did not look up from under the hood but only extended his hand. Ed handed him the wrench he needed. They were working under the hood of a '32 Ford. Once they were sixteen, they had both landed jobs at the filling station pumping gas and working on cars after school. Each day the young men would make their way from school and work at the station until supper time. They also worked a couple of Saturdays each month.

Some of the old gang came around the filling station occasionally, but most had found work to help supplement the family income. Al and Omer worked in the local market. Alfred worked the early morning shift at the bakery. The jobs didn't pay a lot, but it kept some change in their pockets. Most of their pay went to the family for food, clothing, and rent. Things had improved since the beginning of the depression, but not much. The New Deal had not yet reached them.

"Tomorrow's Saturday, Ed. Do you have a date?" asked Punk.

"I only have a date if I double with you because you are the only one with a car so you would know...but no, I don't have a date," said Ed.

"How about we head for the beach? We'll check with the other guys to see if any of them can go and make a day of it."

"I don't think I'm getting a better offer than that. Sure. The boys usually stop by on Fridays so we can check, but I know that Al and Omer work Saturdays at the market and Alfred is always tired from working the early shift at the bakery, so it just might be you and me."

"That's okay," answered Punk looking up and smiling at Ed, "Leaves room in the car for girls."

Punk picked up Ed at about nine the next morning in his '31 Chevy. It wasn't new, but Punk kept it running well. He worked on it at the station every chance he got. They had pretty much stripped it down and rebuilt it but had not replaced any of the interior. The exterior; however, gleamed in the bright sunshine.

They headed out along much the same route as the trolley had taken years before. Since the advent of the popularity of the automobile, many of the small trolley lines had gone out of business. The state still ran the big lines, and the tracks were still in evidence in the roads where the small lines had once carried the masses to work and play. Now it was a jam of cars making their way toward the beach on a warm summer's day.

"The papers say that Cohassett beach is not the same."

"I saw that. Pictures showed plenty of wrecked houses in the 1938 hurricane," said Ed.

"They say most of the amusements are gone; just washed out to sea."

"Didn't they rebuild?"

"I don't think they rebuilt it the same as it was. It was all made from wood and got totally destroyed."

They cruised down Cohassett Beach Avenue and passed St. Rita's Church, just a couple of guys with the world on a string.

"The church looks okay and we're pretty close to the water," said Ed. "How bad could it be?"

"Let's see as we get closer." As they crossed the parkway they could see the carousel building in front of them and that looked fine, but looking to the left and right, many of the small cottages such as the one rented by Obie and Fritch were no longer there. They were supplanted by weedy lots.

They crossed the parkway and made their way toward the beach. The Dodgem building was still there and so was the arcade, doughboy shop, and restaurant; but everything along the waterfront was totally gone. Not that it was damaged or leaning or under repair, it was totally gone. The only remnants that something had stood along the waterfront were a few cement foundations and some sticks poking above the tide line. The trolley bridge to Buttonwoods no longer existed.

"Wow. That must have been one powerful storm."

"They called it the 'Storm of the Century.'"

"Well, it was the 'End of Time' for most of the stuff around here." They parked the car and headed for the beach. The water was as cool as ever and just as refreshing, but something had been lost. The beach no longer rang with the screams of children from the rides or the noise of barkers from the midway. It had taken on an eerie silence like something had died, but no one was sure what time the wake was.

The boys went to the doughboy shop. The doughboy stand had withstood the test of time and the wrath of the storm. They sat at a picnic table with their clam cakes and doughboys as they had a couple of years before.

"The boys would be shocked. This is worse than I ever thought," said Ed looking around.

"I just can't believe it. We used to come down here and we thought it was giant; indestructible."

"Maybe it wasn't that giant, but it sure wasn't big enough to stand against that storm."

"No, Ed. You're right. But there is still the arcade, the carousel, and the dodgems."

Ed and Punk had their fun in the arcade, rode the carousel, and of course took their turn on the dodgems. It was a fine day. They thought about Cohassett Beach and what it had once meant to go there on a Saturday or Sunday afternoon and escape the heat of the city. Neither mentioned it, but there was doubt that it would ever be the same.

As they were leaving, Punk drove through the back streets of the neighborhoods. They saw for themselves that the once merry summer playground would never be as they remembered it. Indeed, many of the cottages and houses were not there to be remembered at all.

Chapter 3: The Way We Were

"Dot, how about we pack-up the kids and go for a ride?" Dot, Ed's wife of 10 years, was just finishing changing the baby and turned from the bassinet brushing hairs back that had stuck to her forehead with sweat.

"It's awfully hot, Ed. Where could we go and cool off a bit? It has been hot all week. Even you said that men were passing out in the factory."

"I know a place. Let's get our stuff together." The apartment was very warm on this Sunday in July and not a breeze was moving in the neighborhood.

Dot and Ed gathered their son, Dennis, and his younger sister Debra and put them in the back of the Desoto and headed south through the city toward Narragansett Bay. Ed drove south heading for a memory of cooler breezes.

The Red Sox were playing, and the fifty-thousand-watt local AM station broadcast the game for all to hear on the radio. Curt Gowdy was calling the play-by-play as the breeze created by the car's movement made it tolerable along the road. Dennis was in the back seat with his hand sticking out the window playing on the breeze and Debra sat in the car seat in the front between Ed and Dot.

Plenty had happened since Ed's last ride with Punk to Cohassett Beach. War had broken out and all the boys had been drafted. Ed had enlisted at seventeen and as he told it walked through North Africa, Sicily, Italy, and France. He had stopped just short of Germany when a minor wound sent him back to England and a headquarters assignment. Miraculously, none of the boys had been killed in the war. Alfred had been wounded but had recovered.

Punk got married and headed off to California to seek his fortune. All the other boys married as well. Ed met Dot. They married and had a son and a daughter. That was an awful lot of water under the bridge. Seventeen years since his trip to Cohassett Beach with Punk and now it was 1956 and he was back. He couldn't say he was the same, but it was just what happened and now he was here.

"Are we there yet?" came the whine from the back seat. The drive had not improved since the last time. The Interstate Highway System was under construction, but not yet operational. But here they were cruising down Cohassett Beach Avenue, passing the familiar St. Rita's Church, and crossing the parkway. At the top of the hill they could smell the doughboys and clam cakes and the popcorn as Ed announced," We're here," to a chorus of cheers from the front and back seat.

The carousel of course was still there along with the doughboy shop, the arcade, and the dodgems. They walked the same sticky sidewalks down to the beach. Dot had brought their swimsuits as a surprise and they changed in the bath house. The children and their parents splashed in the waters of East Greenwich Bay as the boys had long ago before the great storm.

As they rested after their swim, Ed went to the Doughboy stand. As he stood waiting for the order, he gazed east and west along the shore seeing silhouetted in his mind the great midway that had existed when he was a boy. As he thought, he could almost hear the shouts and laughter of children on the amusement rides and the trolley crossing Buttonwoods Cove, the memory vanished as he heard, "Order up!" He took the small box from the counter and returned to the beach with doughboys and clam cakes.

The doughboy for non-New Englanders is a wad of dough dropped in boiling oil until it fries to a golden brown. Then, the fried dough is placed in a bag and shaken with sugar. Those that don't know the treat are surely deprived.

Clam Cakes are a different mixture of cakey batter with clams mixed in. They are also fried in boiling oil and then lightly salted. They are a quickly acquired taste even for those foreign born...out of the New England area.

The group enjoyed their treats, changed back into street clothes, and made their way back up the hill toward what was left of the midway. Debra was too young for any rides and even Dennis was too small for the dodgems but showed interest in a horse race game in the arcade. He watched until he thought he understood and then he and Dad tried their luck.

The object was to flip a lever to lift a ball on a paddle. If you did it exactly right, the ball dropped into a hole and the horse moved along the track. If you missed, the horse didn't move. The first of twelve players to reach the finish line won a carnival prize. There was a good deal of noise including bells and play-by-play of the race by the barker.

Ed and Dennis played twice, losing both times, but making a fair game of it with the other contestants. On the third game, Dennis played alone and won. There was great celebrating all around. The small bear that was the prize made Debra incredibly happy.

They moved on to the carousel where Dad had to accompany Dennis to ride an outside horse, but Dennis couldn't reach the rings no matter how hard he tried. Ed snagged a few rings, but none were brass. Debra rode with Mom in one of the circus carriages. Of course, in those days' parents rode for free with their children.

As the family walked back to the DeSoto, Dennis asked his Dad, "What does that say?" he asked pointing to the facade on building across from the Carousel.

"It says dodgem. It's a ride with cars that bang into each other."

"Don't people get hurt?"

"No. They don't go that fast. They are electric cars and they bang into each other for fun. I used to ride on those with my friends a long time ago."

"I don't know if it sounds like a lot of fun."

"Oh, yes. I remember. Yes, it was a lot of fun. Yes, it was."

Chapter 4: On a Carousel

Donna Reis entered the Sunshine Restaurant on West Shore Road and hesitated by the door obviously looking for someone. Eyes turned toward her as she stopped at the entrance scanning the room. She was a pretty woman with shoulder length auburn hair. This morning she was dressed in fitted jeans with a denim blouse.

Gazing toward the back of the restaurant, she spotted Rulon Drego, the owner of the Ellie's doughboy shop in nearby Cohassett Beach, waving toward her. She returned the wave and moved toward his table and took the seat opposite him. Rulon had jet black hair, slicked back, with just a touch of gray at the sideburns. He was dressed in a sport coat with a starched white shirt open at the throat.

The Sunshine Restaurant is a local breakfast and lunch joint that specializes in good, hot, wholesome food. They have about fifteen tables made with orange Formica seats and is lorded over by two efficient waitresses. One appeared at Donna's shoulder.

"What can I get you?" she asked.

"Just coffee for the moment," Donna replied.

"Oh, get some breakfast, Donna. I've already ordered" Rulon urged.

"Alright, I'll have the special...scrambled."

"Great. I'll be right back with your coffee," said the waitress and she scampered off. Not a minute later she was back with a mug and she poured hot, steaming coffee into it. Donna poured in two creamers and took a sip.

"First, Rulon. As president, I want to thank you for your generous gift to the Carousel Foundation."

"You're welcome, Donna. It's the least I can do. Your dream of bringing a carousel back to Cohassett Beach after all this time is one that I share. I bought the doughboy shop ten years ago in the hopes of bringing back the beach to its former glory. The shop has been successful, but not much else has happened since. Maybe the carousel could help move that revitalization along."

"Well, thank you, Rulon. I hope what you say it true. That is our collective dream for the neighborhood. Just like Crescent Park across the bay in East Providence, we hope to secure grants and the good will of local businessmen, like you, to make this happen."

Their food arrived and they ate as they talked. Rulon had also ordered the special...but over easy on the eggs.

"So, you plan to carve all of the horses for the carousel yourself?" asked Rulon.

"Well, not just me, Rulon. There is a whole organization and we have experts coming in to teach us how it's done. It may take years, but it will also take us some time to find a carousel mechanism to mount the horses and carriages."

"Yes. Yes. That's what I meant. Those are huge undertakings. How long do you think all that might take?"

"I'm thinking five to ten years."

"Wow. That is a long time to sustain the effort. How do you see it ending?"

"Well, I don't know if I can project that far, but it would be nice if we get enough money to get a warehouse or small building to work on and store the horses. Right now, we only have the small place on East Shore Road. All the time we will be on the hunt for a carousel mechanism which we will have to buy and probably restore."

"What about land to put it on?"

"I haven't thought that far yet, but I was hoping the city would let us put it on the common down there at the waterfront or we might acquire a piece of land up near the original location at the top of the hill."

"Well, that certainly is ambitious. I will continue to support your effort, but it will certainly be a long haul."

"I know, but we really appreciate your support and would encourage you to solicit other donors from your business connections."

"I will speak kindly of your organization to others in the hopes they may follow Ellie's Doughboy Shop's lead."

"As I said, I appreciate your support and I am happy that you invited me to breakfast, but you certainly wanted to talk about more than wooden horses."

"I am hurt, Donna," Rulon pouted thumping his chest. "You doubt my philanthropy. I just wanted to solidify the relationship between the Carousel Foundation and Ellie's. Now that we have done that, I do have a bit of a favor to ask."

Donna smiled at him. Rulon was known for his ruthless business sense. Others had tried to muscle in on his monopoly in the beach area and all had failed for one reason or another. She knew there would be a price for his generous donation to the Foundation. She just hoped she could help him and keep the money coming. He was their biggest donor and his continuing support could really get them off the ground.

"I would never ask you to compromise your position in the neighborhood," Rulon began. "You know me better than that, but I do need help with a local matter that I believe is also important to the people of Cohassett Beach. Councilman Elias Fraiser is interested in finding a home for a community center in Cohassett Beach. Other portions of the city have such centers, but we have none."

"That's true, Rulon. Buttonwoods and Pilgrim have a center, why shouldn't we have one in Cohassett Beach?"

"Exactly. Elias is having a hard time convincing other councilmen to commit the funds, but he wants to build a new center. I think he should use the old store front at the top of the hill. If he just remodels that building, the cost would be much lower than building a new center," Rulon pitched his idea.

"That would be a good location and the lower cost surely would help to sell the council on the idea," Donna acknowledged.

"You see my point, then. What we need here is community support for the idea. You have great influence with the members of your foundation. If you could mention it at your meetings and spread the word, I'm sure we could get this done. That piece of land next to the center might be a prime piece for the carousel someday."

"I don't see where that would interfere with the foundation's mission in any way. In fact, it might help to solidify our position and spread the word about the carousel," Donna said and felt she was being truthful, and that Rulon was not asking too much nor was he out of line. That talk about the land next to the storefront building really had her excited.

Rulon smiled at her and wiped his chin with his paper napkin. "Donna you warm my heart. The people of Cohassett Beach will have you to thank when this is a reality. See, that wasn't so painful, was it?" Rulon motioned for the check. "Breakfast is on me. I know your foundation folk don't have an expense account."

"Thank you, Rulon. I hope we can both help Cohassett Beach become a great place to live and work again."

With that Donna gathered her things and made her way for the door giving Rulon a small wave on the way out. Rulon waved back and took his phone from the breast pocket of his sport coat. He was smiling as he punched in the number.

+++++

"Elias."

"Rulon, what a pleasant surprise."

"I just had the most pleasant conversation with Donna Reis."

"Really. Did you talk about her supporting me in the next election?"

"Sort of. We talked about the new community center in Cohassett Beach."

"That's interesting. You know that's one of my pet projects."

"I do, Elias, but you are having a difficult time selling it. I'd like to help you with that; along with Ms. Reis."

"Oh. And how to you propose to do that? Are you going to send over a bunch of doughboys to my next fundraiser?"

"Now. Now, Elias. Let's play nice. Donna is willing to use the Carousel Foundation to rally the neighborhood for your idea."

"Well, that would certainly help…"

"…If you put the center in that storefront at the top of the hill," Rulon broke in.

There was a bit of a pause and Rulon could hear Elias reshuffling his considerable bulk in his big leather chair. "You know, Rulon, that I would like my construction company to build a new center."

" Everybody knows that Elias and that's why you are having trouble getting it by the council. Can't you be satisfied with the remodeling work?"

"Well, if it's between that and nothing…I guess that is better."

"It seems that might be the choice and then everybody gets something."

"You're a shrewd one, Rulon. You should run for office."

"Oh, we wouldn't want that, Elias. Then what would you do?" Rulon hung up, smiled to himself, left a hefty tip for the waitress, and strutted confidently out of the restaurant.

Chapter 5: Puppeteer

"Good afternoon to you all. I'm Brendon Tanner a partner in T & T Real Estate and Development Company. I'm happy you all could make it for lunch today. Every one of you here has some stake in a plan that we would like to present to you this afternoon." Anybody that was anybody in Cohassett Beach or had some financial interest in Cohassett Beach had come with the anticipation that something big would be proposed today. That finally the vacant lots at the beach, mostly vacant since the hurricane of the late 1930's would be developed, and the remaining neighborhood would be revitalized. Mostly they thought that there was plenty of money to be made in the effort.

They had gathered at Sam's Inn a popular watering hole on West Shore road. The lure had been a prime rib luncheon which was known by the locals to be the best around. They had filled their bellies and now wanted to hear how they could fill their wallets.

"Before we get to the specifics of that, I would like to present my partner, Hanley Trent to outline what we want to talk about today; Hanley."

Hanley Trent came to the front of the room carrying a folder. In contrast to his partner, he was a small, thin man. He wore rimless spectacles and had thinning gray hair. Next to his partner, they seemed a Mutt and Jeff team. Brendon looked the manly and foreboding character and Hanley looked the mousey, weak one. This tendency of underestimation had worked well for the partnership as Hanley was as cunning and ruthless as they came.

"Good afternoon. The Cohassett Beach area has long been looked upon as economically depressed. Although some progress has been made in the housing market in the area, the beach just can't seem to break out of the reputation as one of the less attractive and less desirable places to live along with one of the weakest real estate markets. We aim to change all of that," Hanley said holding the folder in front of him like he was nervous speaking to a crowd. The real estate brokers were hoping that the folder contained documents outlining their part in some giant development from which they would squeeze huge profits.

Hanley surely had all their attention. Most of the men in this room had a specific area in which their attention was felt the most. That was the left side of their ass where the bulge was from their fat wallets. The fatter the bulge, the better they liked it and they liked what they were hearing now.

Hanley continued," We have spoken with many of you individually and the support for this project is definitely there," he seemingly made eye contact with each individual in the room and enumerated them with his folder. "We see this project as an infusion of capital, a boon to better housing, and a catalyst for the community to break out of its present doldrums and explode on the real estate market." There was a smattering of applause as bulging wallets were adjusted.

"We have kept most of the planning under wraps in the hopes that the principals could position themselves to anticipate the buying and selling of real estate parcels and to prohibit the gouging of small parcel holders as we garnered the land holdings necessary to initiate the project."

"Does that mean that you could maximize your profits, Hanley," a remark came from the back of the room followed by laughter.

"Something like that, Fred," Hanley smiled and pointed his folder at Fred. Once the room became quiet, Hanley went on. "I don't want to steal all of the thunder here, so I'd like to introduce the principal in this project the former governor of the great state of Rhode Island, Webster Phillips." There was loud applause and many people stood as the popular governor came to the front of the room.

"Thank you. Thank you very much. I came here today because Hanley and Brendon assured me that this would be a friendly crowd. I see many former colleagues and business associates in the group, but to keep Brendon and Hanley's and rest of the T & T Real Estate and Development Company from breaching its trust, I would like to have all weapons checked at the door." This brought a good amount of laughter and groaning as many feigned reaching inside their sport coats and removing their weapons. In a state where *la Familia* was alive and well, some were not feigning.

Ex-governor Phillips stood as tall and handsome as he had when he was elected to two consecutive terms as the leader of state government in landslide votes. He would have won a third term, but state law precluded his running again. Since then he had been involved in a local law firm and worked in real estate development.

"This project is near and dear to my heart and I believe will provide Cohassett Beach with the incentive to revitalize the entire area. The investment we are willing to make represents more than has ever been invested in this area by the city or any other private development." Webster Phillips moved toward a covered easel to the side of where he spoke and with the assistance of Brendon and Hanley lifted the covering.

"Gentlemen, I give you Cohassett Landing." With a flourish they removed the fabric covering. The crowd was quiet. A few of the men got up and came for a closer look at the large, color rendering of the condo/marina project. The murmuring and talking increased. Handshakes were exchanged and there was thunderous applause that went on for several minutes.

Eventually, everyone took their seats and Webster Phillips continued. "As many of you recognize, this is an ambitious plan that requires the acquisition of many small pieces of real estate from developers, the city, and private land holders. Quick movement and complete secrecy are paramount. All the pieces must be in place for the plan to succeed. Without the inclusion of all phases," the governor pointed to the diagram as he spoke, "the condominium development, the parking, store fronts, and the marina; the whole project could collapse under its own weight."

Elias Fraiser, the councilman representing the Cohassett Beach district, stood and addressed the ex-governor. "Governor Phillips, this is indeed a beautiful project. It does represent a revitalization, indeed a gentrification, of the area. Part of the land you require is the two-year old community center which the city spent a great deal of money renovating. I'm not sure we can convince the constituency or the city to give that up."

"Surely you would be willing to build them a new one Elias," Webster Phillips guffawed, and a great deal of laughter followed.

"In all seriousness Governor," it was Bill Debers a local real estate agent. "The city has invested in a basketball court and ball fields that you need for the marina along with the community center. Just the DEM permits for the dredging might prove quite difficult. How do you plan to address those concerns?"

"Thank you for bringing that up Bill. I respect your insight and concern, but we have spoken to the agencies involved and we think we have applied just the right amount of incentive to lead us to believe that we can move forward with the project." He smiled and placed his thumbs into his belt. He looked the picture of confidence. Brandon and Hanley stood by his side and they joined hands and put them in the air in a show of solidarity. There seemed that there was nothing that could stop the project from moving forward.

Rulon Drego looked thoughtful and pensive seated toward the back of the room. If this project were to move forward, would they want a doughboy shop across the street from luxury condominiums; probably not. Would his present parking problem be exacerbated by the new project? And would anyone want a whirling carousel in the midst of this project? He had been invited, but he had not been included in the discussion prior to today. The scope was a complete surprise. Rulon heard there was some development under consideration, but he never thought it was this big. He felt like the odd man out. He had noticed that Donna Reis had not been invited. Her dreams of a carousel might be jeopardized by this project. His own plans might hang in the balance as well along with the community center. Gentrification would surely not support a community center or a doughboy shop.

Webster Phillips waded into the crowd pumping hands as he went and courting support as he did in his gubernatorial campaigns.

"I'm counting on your support with the financing, Alan."

"Sure thing, Governor."

"That lumber contract look good, John?"

"You can count on me, Sir."

"The union boys all on board?"

"We are still in your corner, Governor."

"How are those acquisitions coming along, Bob?"

"Steady and sure, Governor. Steady and sure."

As he got to the exit, Webster Phillips paused and turned to the crowd. "I'm counting on you all and I know you won't let me down. Keep up the good work and we'll all see the promise of this new venture." With that he waved to the crowd and made his way out to the waiting limousine. A young man in a dark suit held an umbrella so that the governor's suit jacket did not get damp.

Rulon made his way over toward Elias Fraiser. The portly man turned when he felt Rulon by his side.

"What do you think, Elias?"

"I don't know if I'm allowed to think. This all seems to be above my pay grade."

"Oh, come now. You've been in bigger fights than this."

"Not with more power than that," Elias said indicating the governor's entourage.

"I noticed Ms. Reis was not among the invited guests. I wouldn't think that there would be room for her here."

"Nor for her flying horse brigade."

"That either."

"We may have some common ground after all, Elias."

"I don't want to commit political suicide over this. You or I can't seem to afford it."

"You may be right. We can't spearhead an effort to kill this project. We'd be massacred in the political street."

"Yes, but we may have a common friend that has the clout to get it done without risk," Rulon suggested.

"I hope so, my friend. I hope so," whispered Elias.

Chapter 6: Sympathy for the Devil

"Mr. Drego. This is Governor Phillips. I'm sorry we didn't have a chance to talk the other day. You may be wondering why you were invited to our little soirée and why I'm calling you now."

"Well, yes Governor. The thought had crossed my mind," said Rulon leaning back in his desk chair.

"Well, don't you worry none. We surely have your best interests in mind. In fact, there is something you can do for me that I would like to discuss. Are you free this afternoon? Say around 2:00?"

"Yes, sir. I am."

"Why don't you come around the office about then and we'll have coffee and talk it over. Does that sound good?"

"Yes, sir; I'll see you at 2:00." And with that the governor hung up.

One of two things was going to happen here, Rulon thought. He is either going to make me an offer to sell out or he needs a favor. Rulon surely didn't want to sell out. Rulon and his family had been operating Ellie's for twenty years now and he did not want to give it up. He had built a brand in the state and was contemplating opening another location and building an upscale restaurant next to his present location. That might not all fit into the governor's plans. As for the favor...that could be anything. The governor was a shrewd manipulator. Rulon would have to be cautious.

+++++++

"Elias. How are you today?"

"Fine, Rulon. Why are you calling me? It seems we are talking a lot lately."

"Well, we have a lot to discuss. The governor just called me."

"The present governor?"

"No, our mutual friend; the great past governor."

"What did that snake want?"

"I don't know. I was hoping you might fill me in on that."

"He doesn't consult with me. I'm going to lose my balls over this new deal. My fellow council members and my constituency are going to smell a rat over this community center thing no matter what I say. I'm stuck in a corner."

"That is precisely where I don't want to be. He wants to see me at 2:00 this afternoon."

"Watch out for that SOB, Rulon. We think we're shrewd, but he is a master. Don't let him extract promises that you can't keep. You might as well just fall on your sword."

"I'll try to be careful. I'll let you know what I find out. Talk to you later."

"I hope so. Good luck, Rulon."

Well, that was no help. If Elias didn't know the local maneuvering, no one did. This was a big money project and required state and city agency deals to get the right permits. The right people would have to be greased. Rulon knew the locals, but the state was another matter.

+++++++

"The Governor will see you now." The receptionist smiled at Rulon gracefully and indicated the door to her right as she stood and opened it for him. Rulon passed close by her. She smelled good and looked better, but the smile was a business one and indicated no warmth. It disappeared as soon as he passed.

"Come in, Rulon. Come in. Have a seat." The Governor indicated a seat in front of his desk. The visitor's chairs were indeed comfortable, and the real leather squeaked as Rulon sat. "Can I get you anything? Coffee? Tea? A little early for me, but something stronger?"

"Coffee will be fine, Governor."

Webster Phillips reached for a button on his desktop phone. "Brenda, could you bring us two coffees please? Thank you."

Brenda promptly brought in two coffees on a tray and set it on the table in front in the sitting area.

"Let's move over here." The Governor rose and moved to the sitting area. The Governor took the chair; that left the couch for Rulon. They both sat back and sampled their coffee.

"Is it alright for you?"

"Fine Governor. Fine."

"I have been down to your establishment and you do put out some fine food. I especially like your red clam chowder."

"Thank you, Governor. It has been voted best in the state: twice."

"Well deserved. Well deserved."

"And it looks like you do quite well with that business if the state income tax forms can be believed."

"Yes sir. We have worked extremely hard to make it a success." The Governor had probably had his people review all of Rulon's accounts. He probably knew them better than Rulon did.

"And it looks like you are well entrenched at your present location."

Alright, here it comes. He's buttered me up and now here comes the offer I can't refuse.

"Yes, sir. We have built up a loyal following over the years."

"I need something that might prove a bit sticky for you to deliver."

"What's that sir?"

"I need Elias Fraiser to support this project. He has the following to swing the locals in our favor. If the area prospers, his constituency prospers."

"I can't speak for him sir, but his constituency may not see it that way."

"What can't they see? This is a development on a grand scale. Their property values will go up," the governor pointed out.

"That's just it, Sir. We are talking about blue collar workers here. Many of those people live paycheck to paycheck and can barely afford their homes now. If their property values increase, their taxes will go up and they may be priced out of their own homes."

"Nonsense. This development will improve the neighborhood. Once it's done, they will see that."

"Maybe, but they can't see it now. They may only see that their access to the waterfront is being restricted and they are losing a good part of their beach to the marina. The clam diggers will lose their dock space and in their eyes their livelihood."

"But if Elias comes out in support of the development, doesn't he have the clout to swing the voters?"

"Maybe, but it will cost him. He would need monetary and other support in the next election to swing the vote back his way. The voters may not forgive his transgression."

"Sure. Sure. We can help him out there. Will you approach him? If it looks like I am applying the pressure, it won't look good."

"Yes sir. I can ask and deliver your message of future support if I get your meaning."

"Yes. Yes. You can tell him that. If he doesn't feel he can come right out and support the project for the reasons you outlined, what if he just remains neutral?"

"I think I can promise neutrality more than support. I will talk to him as you asked and deliver the entire message."

"I would appreciate that and good luck with your business." The Governor rose and Rulon felt that he was dismissed. They shook hands and the Governor opened the door and bade him a good day.

+++++++

"Elias, he wants your public support on the project," Rulon said into the telephone.

"That is political suicide for me. He must know that. He's got my balls in a vice. If I support him, I get his support in return and that means a lot, but if I do support this project I lose all of my political capital and even his support might not be able to buy it back. I'm fucked."

"Maybe not, Elias. You may be able to remain neutral and not seem like you're giving in. He said that would be enough...at least that you do not oppose the project."

"If I say nothing, my voters will see that as support. They expect me to fight for them. That's what won me this job in the first place."

"Well, maybe we can get someone else to fight this for us. We keep our mouths shut publically and the Governor thinks we are with him. If we can get someone to fight this as a proxy for us, we could come out smelling like a rose," suggested Rulon.

"More like a pile of manure the way things are going. Who's man enough to bail us out of this?"

"Not man enough, Elias, but a woman."

Chapter 7: The Heart of the Matter

Russ Deever and Sophia Fleming live in a condo about ¾ of a mile from Cohassett Beach. They have been together for over a year. Sophia is a teacher at the local elementary school and Russ is a detective in the Warwick Police department. Russ went to law school nights and weekends. He passed the bar last year, but presently is a Detective Sergeant for the Warwick Police Department.

Russ is also retired Army with most of his time spent in the National Guard. He met Sophia because she lived in the same apartment building and she looked great in a jogging suit. Last year she gave up her apartment and moved into his place.

Russ stirred and sat up in bed.

"Honey." He heard from deep below the covers. "Are you getting up?"

"I was thinking about it. Why? When we were in Ogunquit, you were up before dawn waiting for the sunrise over the ocean."

"That was then, now you can make the coffee." And then the lump next to him turned over.

"Sure, no problem." He yanked the covers with him as he rose from the bed and left the bedroom.

"Hey!" was all he heard in response from the now uncovered Sophia followed by a pillow to the back of the head. He turned and made a dive on to the bed smothering her with the blankets.

"Ooo that's bet..." Nothing more escaped her lips as he covered her mouth with his. "Mmm, I could do with more of that…" she said, and he kissed her again. Within a few moments they were pulling at each other's night clothes and you might say they were in a tight bond.

"Naughty girls get punished," Russ whispered in her ear.

"I'll have to learn how to be naughtier than," and she buried her face in his chest and wrapped her legs around his torso.

After a few moments they were spent and lay back catching their breath.

"I need to go to the bathroom," Sophia said getting up and over doing it with a sexy walk on the way. A pillow hit her in the back of the head as she reached the door.

"And seeing as you're up…make the coffee." Russ caught the pillow as she hurled it back at him.

When the coffee was done, Russ and Sophia were sitting on the second-floor balcony enjoying the warmth of the sun on a Saturday morning. As was his habit, Russ was reading the paper.

"Hey, The Cohassett Beach Café is open again and serving breakfast."

"Isn't that the biker bar?"

"It was, but not anymore. After the last incident, a few months ago, they lost their liquor license. It says they are open under new management. Should we try it?"

"If you will walk down to the beach with me?" Sophia walked every morning and she was always coaxing Russ to go with her. He seldom did.

"So, that is my price for offering to buy you breakfast. I have to walk."

"Seems you were happy with exercising a few minutes ago; how about we continue that program?"

"I didn't know that this was a continuing program, but you win. I'll walk to the beach with you." They quickly prepped and walked the fifteen minutes down the avenue to the café. There were a few patrons, leaving plenty of seats available.

The new owner had redecorated. There were fresh curtains in the windows and the place had a fresh coat of paint. It looked very festive with alternating red and white tablecloths.

"Good morning. I'm Holly Richards the new owner. Welcome to the Cohassett Beach Café." She greeted them at the door as they entered the restaurant.

"Wow. This place sure looks different from the last time I was here," Russ remarked looking around.

"When was the last time you were here?" Holly asked. Holly was of medium height with short black hair. She wore a yellow blouse and a black skirt. She was feminine but looked like she could handle herself if someone tried to push her around.

"About eight months ago I responded to a call about a brawl here in the bar. The place was quite torn up and sure didn't look this nice even before the brawl." Russ realized that of course Holly had no idea who he was. "Sorry, I'm Russ Deever and this is Sophia. I work as a detective for the Warwick Police and Sophia teaches at the local elementary school."

"Well. It's always good to meet Warwick's finest and it's nice to me you Sophia. I don't think I could teach kids. It must be exhausting. Welcome to the Cohassett Beach Café. Right this way." They followed Holly and were seated at a table by a window. "Coffee?"

They both indicated they would, and Holly left them with menus.

"This place really does look great," Russ said as they were perusing the menus.

"I've never been in here before. It seems nice."

"It wasn't so nice before. The clientele was a bit rough. If you had been here before you would probably have a couple of tattoos; some of which would only be in places that I have seen."

"No, not exactly my style."

Their waitress came by and they ordered. While they waited, they made small talk.

"They say the beach was quite the place in its heyday," said Sophia. "I didn't know much about it before I moved here and started walking in the morning. This is part of my usual route."

"That's what I'm told. I only came here as a boy with my family. Most of the amusements were gone by then, destroyed by the hurricane. I see there are some old pictures on the walls in here. All I remember is the carousel, the doughboy shop, and the arcade. That building across the street," Russ indicated the apartment building across the street from where they were sitting, "Used to house the dodgem cars. Did you ever come down here with your folks?"

"No. This wasn't one of our haunts. We went more to Crescent Park in East Providence. You know; they put an old carousel back in there a few years ago."

"Yes, I've seen that. They want to do the same thing here, but it is slow in coming. They are working on carving horses, but they don't have a mechanism as yet."

"I've seen their shop on East Shore Road. It would be a nice addition to the beach if they could get that done."

Their breakfast arrived and they ate hungrily. As they were finishing, Holly came over.

"How was everything?"

"Very good, thanks," they both answered.

"So, how have things been going?" Sophia asked.

"We have only been open two weeks, but the word is getting out and business is improving every day."

"That's good to hear. We have so many good restaurants here in Warwick that the competition is fierce."

"That's true, but we think there is a niche we can fill here down at the beach; especially with the summer crowd."

"Well, we wish you good luck."

Holly walked outside with Sophia and Russ to the parking lot. When the couple made for the sidewalk Holly asked. "Where is your car?"

"Oh, we didn't use a car. We live in a condo about a mile up the avenue, so we just walked."

"That's right. Sophia promised me breakfast if we walked, so I took her up on it."

"You should do that more often."

"We would love to." Russ promised. "Sophia, have I ever showed you the cement foundation from the old carousel here in the parking lot?"

"Where?"

"Yes, where," added Holly.

"You are standing right in it. See the ten-foot, dirt circle in the middle and the wider cement circle showing where the doors were and the round sidewalk most of the way around?" Russ turned and pointed to the remainder of the circular cement foundation of the old carousel as he spoke. "You can almost hear the music of the carousel if you listen really close."

"Well, I don't hear any music, buddy boy, but I do see the formations you're talking about. If you're done reminiscing about your childhood, maybe we should get going. Holly has work to do."

"No. No. I didn't know what those cement pieces were. That's great to know. Now I can tell my customers we are on the site of the old carousel. Well, hello Rulon." Holly turned to greet Rulon Drego who had walked the block from his doughboy shop up the hill to the Cohassett Beach Café."

"Hello, Holly. Officer…err…I don't recall your name."

"Russ Deever and its detective. This is Sophia."

Rulon nodded toward Sophia. "Of course," Rulon said shaking Russ's hand. "I should have remembered. We met that time you responded to a problem we had down at the doughboy shop."

"Of course." Russ said. "I trust you have not had any problems since."

"No; and thank you for your help that day. It was greatly appreciated."

"No thanks necessary...that's why we're here."

"Shouldn't we get going, Russ?" Sophia prodded.

"Yes. Nice meeting you Holly and nice seeing you again Mr. Drego." And with that they started walking back toward their condo.

"Let's walk along the water rather than up the avenue" said Sophia.

"It figures. You get me to take the long way home."

"But it's so nice to walk along the water. There is so much more to see..."

"And you get me to walk more..."

"That's so you can walk off that hash you had with breakfast." And they moved along down the parkway.

Rulon and Holly waved toward the departing couple. When they were out of earshot Holly turned to Rulon. "What brings you up the street Mr. Drego?"

"Oh, Holly. Call me Rulon. Can't a fellow business owner come to say hello."

"Seldom do you come just to say hello, Rulon. What do you want?"

"I was just wondering how you were doing opening for breakfast?"

"I think it has been worth it so far. We'll have to see how it goes in the coming weeks."

"That's good to hear."

"I know you're not thrilled that I re-opened the restaurant Rulon, but I don't think we are in competition."

"I don't wish you ill, Holly. It's just that I had some other ideas, but now that you're here...that's just the way it is."

Holly had spoken with Rulon before and she understood he was not thrilled with her for opening the café. She was sure that he had made it difficult for her to obtain the necessary permits. The two-week parking study that the city had required...she was sure that was also his idea. There were several hoops that she was sure were being controlled by Rulon, but in the end, he could not block her opening. Rulon was a local political force to be reckoned with.

"I see you have discovered the ghosts of the old carousel on your property," Rulon said indicating the cement foundations that Russ had shown her.

"Yes, Russ...Detective Deever, pointed it out to me."

"You should be wary of ghosts...they can haunt you. Have a nice day, Holly."

With that Rulon turned and walked back toward his shop. Holly looked again at the old cement blocks outlining the carousel. She wondered if indeed the old ghosts would reclaim what was once theirs.

Chapter 8: Get Off of My Cloud

"Resendez...Deever...get in here," bellowed Captain Marep from his office echoing through the squad room.

"Let's go Carl," said Russ. "Sounds like the Captain has something for us." Russ and Carl, the lead detective partners on the shift, got up and headed for the Captain's office.

"Looks like we're up. Must be important," said Carl jumping from his desk chair.

"I'm sure we're going to find out soon enough," Russ said leading Carl into the Captain's office.

"Shut the door and have a seat," said Captain Marep; all the while continuing to work on some papers in front of him. The detectives sat and waited. When the Captain had finished, he signed the reports, placed them in the out basket, and picked up a file folder from the front of his desk. He opened it slowly and examined the one sheet of paper with a sticky note attached that it contained while he slowly rubbed the perspiration from his bald head.

"I have something I need you to handle very delicately. I got a call from the Mayor's office." The Captain continued to rub his head as if hoping for a genie to appear or the thought to go away. "It seems the mayor has received a few calls from some locals over in the Cohassett Beach area about the trash from Ellie's Doughboy Shop and customers parking on lawns and sidewalks."

"Do you want us to go and tag cars, Captain?" Carl asked.

The Captain shook his head. "This is a sensitive matter, Carl. I need you two to go down and see Rulon Drego, the owner of the shop, and explain the situation," he made a smoothing motion with his hands as if he were calming the waters of a raging sea. "Mr. Drego needs to get control of his patrons somehow before the city takes action against his establishment. Don't threaten him...just advise him that he might ask his patrons to be a little more considerate of the neighborhood. Maybe put up some signs or something. Put out a few more trash cans...I don't know...get creative...you know what I mean."

"Solve a problem before someone solves it for him," suggested Russ.

"I wouldn't put it so bluntly, but yes" the Captain said looking somewhat relieved.

"I think I understand Captain. We'll see what we can do."

"The Mayor asked me to do this personally so don't fuck it up. Okay?"

"Yes, sir. We'll do our best."

"Dismissed. Let me know how it goes."

"Yes, sir." With that the pair of detectives left the Captain's office.

+++++++

As they drove toward Cohassett Beach Russ suggested, "Carl, let me do most of the talking. We'll get some lunch and sit in the restaurant section of Ellie's and see if Drego comes out or maybe we can catch his eye, so it doesn't seem like we came in just to see him."

"Like it's just a casual meet up."

"Yeah, you got the idea. We don't want to get him all riled so that he calls the mayor and gets us and the Captain in hot water."

"You're the lawyer. Do your counseling thing."

"Okay. Here we are. They joined the line out on the sidewalk and placed their lunch order. Rulon saw them through the window and waved, so he knew they were there. Chances are he would come out and talk if he wasn't too busy. They didn't have to wait long. Russ and Carl took seats at one of the picnic tables and Drego joined them about ten minutes later.

"Detectives. It is good to see you. Keeps the clientele in order," Rulon said wiping his hands on a dish towel.

"Nice to see you too, Mr. Drego."

"To what do I owe this honor or do you just like the food?"

"Oh, we like the food, but we do have something to discuss. It is sort of official/unofficial business" said Russ.

"What? Are you selling union raffle tickets?"

"No, nothing like that," said Russ. "We have had some, err, complaints and we wanted to share them with you."

"Complaints...about what?" Drego seemed to be getting upset.

"Mr. Drego...please take this in the spirit in which it is meant. We do not want to start any trouble for you. We are here on friendly terms. Please...we just want to apprise you of a problem; not accuse or threaten."

Drego looked out over the bay waters and then took a seat at the picnic table with Russ and Carl. "Okay, Detectives. Let's hear what you got to say." Drego seemed to have calmed somewhat and gave the impression that he might be more receptive.

"As I said, there have been some complaints," continued Russ. "The first is about parking. Some people in the neighborhood have called in that some restaurant patrons are parking on their sidewalks and lawns."

"What am I supposed to do about that?" Rulon said spreading his arms wide. "Many people who come here on the weekend are going to the beach along with buying food here so it's really a city problem not just mine."

"That may be true, but we are looking for creative solutions, here."

"Like...?"

"Maybe some signs in the windows reminding people about parking on private property or just passing the word."

"We could try something like that, but I'm not sure it would work."

"Mr. Drego, if it just helped a little, it would be an improvement and people might back off," added Carl.

"That's right. As long as the streets are passable for fire and police..." said Russ.

"I see your point. I'll see what I can do. You said there were complaints...meaning more than one," stated Rulon. "Let's have it."

"The other problem is trash," said Russ.

"Trash...what the hell am I supposed to do about trash. The city receptacles are too small, and they overflow on the weekends. Maybe you should talk to your parks and recreation people. Jeez, trash," Rulon said shaking his head.

"You have to admit, Mr. Drego, that the trash containers would accommodate normal beach trash if it wasn't for the refuse generated by Styrofoam food containers...mostly from your restaurant. Maybe a few more trash cans outside the doughboy shop would help?"

"It's always me. Why do I have to shoulder the responsibility?"

"In my travels, many communities make local businesses supply and empty their own trash containers. We're just asking for a little help here before this becomes an issue."

Okay. Okay. You win. I'll get some more barrels and put them out front and in the parking lot."

"That's the spirit. If the businesses cooperate maybe, we can keep the area looking good and that has to be better for everyone."

"I suppose you're right. Is that it?"

"That's it. Thanks for your time Mr. Drego," Russ shook Rulon's hand.

"Thanks, Mr. Drego; by the way, I really enjoyed the chowder and clam cakes...best I ever had," remarked Carl also shaking Rulon's hand.

"Best in the state," boasted Rulon, "Two years running."

+++++++

"What in the fuck is going on, Elias? I just had two cops here telling me that they have had complaints about parking and trash. And they expect me to fix it. They said they were just being friendly. Jeez, Elias, I pay big money in taxes, don't I get services, too?"

Elias was holding the phone away from his ear Rulon was yelling so loudly. Now that Rulon had taken a breath, maybe he could calm him down. "Take it easy, Rulon."

"Take it easy. All you can say is...take it easy. What the hell am I supposed to do about where people park?"

Elias took a deep breath. Rulon was not going to be happy about what he was going to tell him. "Rulon, this is not the first I've heard about this. The council has discussed both issues in executive session."

"Why didn't you tell me before?"

"Because I knew you would react just like this."

Rulon sat back in his office chair. Now he was on the defensive and was unsure about what to do. "Okay, Elias. What do you suggest?"

"I suggest you try to nip this in the bud as the officers suggested. A few more trash cans and a few signs might do the trick. The alternative is not pretty."

"Alternative! What alternative" asked Rulon. Elias grimaced and held the phone away from his ear once more.

Elias was forever the politician and wanted this problem to go away, but he would first have to convince Rulon that taking action was in his own best interest. "The solutions that the council has discussed are not exactly business friendly, if you know what I mean?"

"I'm not sure I do, Elias."

"Well, they have been talking about a parking ordinance prohibiting on street parking in the Cohassett Beach area and even charging for parking at the beach lot. There also has been some discussion of turning the trash pickup over to the local businesses. You know they do that in some places."

"So, I've heard. Charging for parking and a parking restriction would be a disaster for the doughboy shop." Rulon's voice was now much quieter as he was becoming amenable to a solution that would make this all better. The alternative would be a disaster.

"I've been telling you for some time that you need more parking. You said you were going to buy that empty lot next to Ellie's...did you ever do it?"

"Not yet."

"It might be time to make a move. Especially, if you ever wanted to expand to a sit-down restaurant like you talked about. The zoning board would never approve your opening more restaurant space without more parking. You should have bought that café when you had the chance."

"Okay, Elias. I get the picture. Thanks." Rulon's brain was now in full "fix it" mode. He was calmer and saw that he would have to make this go away.

Elias let Rulon think and convince himself to see reason. He changed the subject after a moment. "Have you talked to our mutual friend about helping us out with that project yet?"

"What?"

"Remember stopping that building we don't want across the street from you?"

"Right; I'll get right on that. And thanks for the information. It looks like I have some maneuvering to do. By the way, do you know where I can pick up some trash cans...cheap?"

Elias was laughing as he hung up the phone.

Chapter 9: The Pusher

Rulon Drego turned his black, shiny Mazda MX-5 with the red seats into a parking space in front of the Carousel Foundation's new headquarters on East Shore Road. He had the top down on the sleek convertible so he could welcome the approving stares as he drove the streets of Cohassett Beach. The day was sunny and dry with no rain in the forecast.

Rulon hopped out of the car and straightened his sport coat and tie as he approached the store window. He paused a moment to admire two of the carousel horses displayed along with admiring his own reflection in the storefront window. The carved horses were brightly colored and exquisite in their detail. Rulon though they were quite beautiful. He opened the door and a small bell tinkled attached to the top of the door.

"Hello," Rulon called in a raised voice. He was in a front area that had a counter and a small table displaying pictures of carved horses and circus carriages. The walls were also covered with pictures of more carvings in various stages of their production. "Hello," he called again and then noticed a button on the counter that said *ring for service.* He pressed it. The power tools he could hear working behind the wall quieted and he heard footsteps approaching.

"Rulon; so nice to see you," said Donna Reis removing her goggles as she came through the doorway. "What brings you to our shop?" She was dressed in a t-shirt and jeans, her usual attire. She wore a blue carpenter's apron and was covered with wood shavings and saw dust. "Excuse my appearance, but this is what we do here." There were more tool noises coming from the back.

"Good to see you Donna. I can tell you are not alone."

"No. Jim Falmer is here helping me today."

"Could I have a peek at the new operation?"

"Why sure. Come around the counter and follow me to the back." They made their way to the warehouse space behind the store front. The Carousel Foundation had recently moved from their rather small location to this larger building. The first space behind the front "office" was the workshop. There were several horses in various stages of completion attached to benches and surrounded by tools. Jim Falmer was working on a wooden horse at one of the stations. He put down his tools and removed his goggles as they approached.

"Hello there, Rulon. What brings you around?" Jim asked. Jim was similarly dressed to Donna in a carpenter's apron.

"Just checking where my money is going. It looks like great progress has been made since the move."

"In the old location," Donna said, "We could only work on two or three horses at a time. In this space we can work on seven or eight."

"Where do you store the finished products?"

"Follow me," said Donna and she moved to the rear of the workspace and through a closed door. "This is the paint room. We hand paint all of the horses right here in the shop." There were two horses and one carriage being worked on in this area. "Let's keep going." Donna walked through another door and Jim and Rulon followed.

"This is our warehouse space. Donna proudly waved her hand. There was a dozen or more pieces completed each covered with plastic. They were magnificent in their workmanship and coloring.

"These are fantastic," remarked Rulon. "It looks like you are almost done."

"Well, not quite. Including the carvings in work we have about 75% of the carvings completed or nearing completion. In about eight months, we will have all of the horses and carriages done."

"Wow; quite an accomplishment. Three years ago, I would not have believed you could do it. But look at you now."

"It's not just me Rulon. We have several donors, such as you, to thank and at least one hundred people have worked on the carvings over the years."

"What about a mechanism. Have you had any luck in finding that?"

"Yes. We are extremely excited. In the last few weeks, we got a line on two carousels in storage: one in California and one in Wisconsin. We are very hopeful."

"Good for you. Good luck in picking one of those up."

"They won't be cheap," added Jim. "We'll need a big fundraising push to get us over the top."

"You have gotten the project this far. I'm sure when people see how close you are, they will be more than willing to donate what you need."

"There will be a lot of work left to rebuild and refurbish the mechanics. That will probably take another year. We will need different skills to get that done. Carvers and painters are not machinists."

"I don't doubt that it will happen. You're almost there," said Rulon.

"Except for the land," sighed Donna. "The city will not budge on the waterfront. They put up the two gazebos and now there isn't enough room for the carousel on the waterfront. They just don't want to hear it."

"Well, as I indicated before, maybe I can help you with that."

"But how? The café is now open and appears to be doing well. There is no land for the carousel available; at least not on the beachfront."

"There is land, but it is destined to become something else that might doom your project forever."

"Whatever do you mean?"

"I hear, and this is all very hush-hush, that the land across from the café is slated for condominium development. They also want to put in a marina."

"What! You mean that Governor Phillips is still chasing that pipe dream? I thought that died a while ago," said Jim with his hands on his hips.

"I heard that all of the land on the east side of the street, including the community center would be cleared right down to the waterfront. The condos would be built on the high ground and the lower ground would be dredged for a marina. The project is very much alive, and they are ready to break ground."

"That would destroy the ball fields, the community center, and the docks used by the fishermen," stated Jim. "I never thought that would fly."

"I'm told the project is all set. Everything is in place with a completion date of two years from now," said Rulon matter-of-factly.

"How did you find out about it," asked Donna.

"I was looking to buy the lot next to the community center for additional parking and that's how I found out that the project was a go," said Rulon. It wasn't exactly true, but it really didn't matter to the Carousel Foundation how he found out and it would serve to cover the real story for now.

"All of those houses, the docks, the community center, and the fields...all turned into a playground for the gentry. I can't believe the city is going along with that," said Jim shaking his head in disbelief.

"Oh, you better believe it. According to my source, the permits are in place, the city is on board, and once it starts...well, no one is going to stop it," Rulon said. "It's a sad state and I know it's something you didn't want to hear..."

"The shovels aren't in the ground yet. When is the next city council meeting?" asked Donna.

"A week from Wednesday," answered Jim.

"We have a foundation meeting tomorrow night. Let's see what our people think of this," said Donna. Turning to Rulon she said, "Thanks for telling us about this. I don't know if we can stop it, but we can sure put up a stink."

"Easy, Donna. You can't say you heard this from me. This is big money and power we're talking about behind this project."

"Don't worry, Rulon. We'll keep you out of it. Jim let's hit the phones and make sure everyone comes to the meeting. Thanks again, Rulon."

"You're welcome, Donna...Jim...have a good day." And with that Rulon showed himself out. As he got back into the convertible he put on his sunglasses, started the car, and smiled as he pulled out very satisfied with himself.

Chapter 10: The Hard Way

After his talk with Donna and Jim, Rulon was feeling a bit smug. The ball was rolling and rolling in his favor. Elias would be pleased at the city council meeting when Donna raised a fury over the marina project. Other residents would surely support her and oppose the marina once the word was out.

The day was certainly magnificent; sunny and bright with the wind blowing through his hair as Rulon drove his car through town. Passersby waved at him and he confidently waved back. Rulon was feeling sure that things were certainly going his way, but you can't ever be too sure.

Rulon had these political matters clouding his mind as he pulled into the local New York System hot wiener shop. He parked the car and strode into the shop, straightening his tie and waving to someone he knew at the counter before taking a seat at one of the tables.

It was a small restaurant that specialized in lunch, especially hot wieners. Any self-respecting New Englander would never call them hot dogs. They were not hot dogs. They were a bit smaller and spicy and when you got a yearning for them, a New York System shop was the only place to go.

"Hey, Rulon. What can I get you?" asked Connie. Connie had big, bleach-blond hair with breasts bursting forth from her waitress uniform which strained to contain her hips. She had red nails that resembled talons and Rulon was sure she knew how to use them. Her lips matched her nails and her eye make-up was heavy. She was poised with her pencil and order pad.

"Hi, Connie. Three all the way with a coffee milk," answered Rulon.

"Three all-the-way with a coffee milk," Connie bellowed half-turning toward the counter. She also made a note on her pad.

For non-aficionados, hot wieners are a northeast delicacy. They are a small, spicy "hot dog" served on a steamed wiener roll. All-the-way refers to the preparation for the purist...that is...mustard, wiener sauce, and onions. The wiener sauce is a concoction of hamburger, tomato, and spices that can burn the stomach lining of a non-believer. The coffee milk is the elixir that will quell the rumble from the standard three-pack of culinary delights that now appeared on a white paper plate in front of Rulon.

"Here you go, hon," Connie said as she delivered his order. "Have a nice day," she concluded slapping the check face down on the table next to his paper plate.

"Thanks, Connie," Rulon replied picking up the first wiener and taking a huge bite. He didn't indulge in this sort of lunch very often, but he surely was savoring every bite chasing it all down with the large cup of coffee milk.

"What's shakin' Rulon?" a man with a thin moustache said sitting down at the table. "How have you been?"

"Frankie! How are things, man?" Rulon said wiping his mouth with a napkin and shaking the man's hand. "Who's your friend?" Frankie had brought another man to his table. He was clean shaven and standing by the table like he was waiting for an invitation.

"This is my friend, Dave. Dave, pull up a chair," said Frankie. Dave got a chair from another table and joined the group. "Dave, this is Mr. Rulon Drego. He owns Ellie's Doughboy shop down at the beach. We went to high school together."

"Hello Mr. Drego."

"Hi, Dave," Rulon answered. "So, what's been going on?" Rulon asked turning back to Frankie.

"Not much," said Frankie. "There hasn't been much work since we got out of the joint."

"Oh, that's right. You got sent up for the Big Ern drug caper. What did you get; two years?" Frankie and Dave had received their sentence for transporting cocaine and heroin across state lines. They had picked up cars in Long Island, New York, and ferried them to Big Ern's car dealership in Rhode Island. From there the drugs were distributed via a system of car parts delivery vans and convenience stores. The Warwick Police had busted the ring. It had made the front page of the Providence Journal when it went down and during the trial.

"We served 18 months with time off," said Frankie "Big Ern is still in the joint."

"That sure was a big hullabaloo. It made all the papers."

"Yeah, the pictures were great," said Frankie brushing it off and trying to change the subject. "Rulon, we need some work. You know how it is with a record."

"I understand, but you guys are a bit hot." Rulon sat back and thought. He finished his coffee milk and wiped his mouth with the paper napkin once more. He knew Frankie had a crew. Maybe he could use them to put some pressure on Holly to abandon the café. She was doing okay, but business wasn't that great. With a little push, maybe she would give it up and Rulon could solve his parking problem once and for all; no matter what happened with the marina project. He could cover his bet both ways. "Maybe I do have something you could do for me."

"We sure would appreciate it, Rulon. Things have been tough, and we need some quick cash."

Rulon took a roll of cash from his pocket and peeled off a $20 bill and left it on the table to cover the bill. "Why don't you walk with me outside?" Rulon stood and made his way toward the door. "Have a good day Connie," and he waved as Frankie and Dave followed him out to the parking lot.

Once they were outside in the bright sunshine and away from prying eyes and ears, Rulon spoke to Frankie. Dave leaned in and listened intently but didn't say anything. "I think I may have something you can help me with. First, take a few bucks as a down payment...shall we say for service rendered." Rulon peeled off a couple of twenties and handed them to Frankie as he shook his hand. "There is a restaurant at the beach called the Cohassett Beach Café."

"You mean the old biker bar," said Dave.

"He speaks. Yeah, that's the place although it isn't a biker bar anymore. The woman who runs the place is insistent on making it a success. I would rather that didn't happen. You know what I mean?"

"Kind of disrupt the flow of things so to speak?"

"Yeah...like that. Small things...you know. Just so as the clientele becomes...shall we say disenchanted with the place."

"I got it...maybe a couple of small accidents."

"Just so as nobody notices that it's on purpose and nobody gets hurt," Rulon whispered.

"Right..."

Rulon hopped in his car and left a small patch of rubber as he exited the parking lot. He looked down and noticed he had dripped mustard and wiener sauce on his shirt.

Chapter 11: Wide-Open Spaces

"Rulon, what can I do for you?" Bill Debers said picking up the phone. Bill owned a one-man real estate company in the Cohassett Beach area. He eked out a living renting houses and occasionally selling one. His office was on East Shore Road in a strip mall about a block away from the Carousel Foundation.

"Hi, Bill. I need some help acquiring some land that I can use for parking for the doughboy shop. The town fathers are on my ass; so, I have to move quickly. I'm interested in the two lots on the north side to the shop between Ellie's and the cafe. The property has been abandoned for years. I'm not even sure who owns it. Could you find out and get back to me?"

"Of course. I think they are still owned by the original family that owned businesses that used to be there back in the day but got destroyed in the hurricane. I'll have to find out who the principals are; could take a few days or weeks." Bill could hear Rulon's intake of breath on the other end of the phone.

"This is getting a bit urgent, Bill. I've already heard some whispers about parking regulations. If I don't nip this soon, my customers won't have anywhere to park and that won't be good for business."

"I understand, Rulon. I'll see what I can do...and move as quickly as can."

"Thanks, Bill. I would appreciate all you can do for me. Talk to you soon." With that the connection was broken.

If this didn't happen soon and he wasn't sure it would, he might have to come up with an alternate plan. He hated to do it, but maybe he could lease some space from Holly. Holly controlled two lots, one on either side of her building, which was more than she needed as parking for her restaurant. Maybe if he offered her the right price, she would bite. He would have to try.

+++++++

"Rulon! Welcome to the Cohassett Beach Café," Holly greeted him as he came in the door at lunchtime a few days later. "Would you like a table or have you just come to gloat?"

"A table please. Gloat about what?"

Holly escorted Rulon to a table and set down a menu for him. He sat and she took the chair opposite his.

"Gloat about my not doing well. Has the word spread?"

"Well, it has now." Maybe this would be easier than he had anticipated. If Holly was desperate for cash, she might go for a deal to lease the lot and maybe for less than he had thought.

"It's just been a struggle," Holly said slumping her shoulders.

"Every new restaurant is a struggle," Rulon said. "Everyone thinks it's easy. Make food...everybody has to eat...they pay you...you make money."

"That's just it. I need bigger numbers. Why don't they come?"

"Because there are a hundred other places they can go. And they can't come to the same one every day or every week. People like variety. If you get them a couple of times a month, you are lucky. So, you need a lot of customers. More than anyone ever thinks. Word of mouth advertising takes a long time," Rulon continued. "Radio, TV, and newspapers help. Specials help and coupons help, but it all comes down to the number of people and the frequency. For every new customer you get, someone else loses them...at least for that day. It's a rough business."

"Why have you been so successful?"

"It hasn't always been easy, but I have the beach customers. Doughboys, clam cakes, and fries; those are snacks. People don't even have to be hungry to buy those. The meals for me are a bonus. Put it all together and it's good, but it is a constant struggle. You see my ads in the paper and on TV and radio; those aren't cheap, but it is the only way to keep it going."

"I'm just getting a bit tired; that's all. I'll bounce back. It's been a tough week."

"Maybe we can help each other out," Rulon offered. She looked at him, but he knew she did not trust him. "I have a problem and you have a problem. We have been discussing yours. Let's discuss mine."

"What problems could you have?"

"My problem is parking," Rulon admitted. "I only have a small lot and people have to park on the streets and in the beach lot. That means they must walk a long way to get their food. That's not good for business." Holly didn't need to know about the complaints the neighbors had filed. The lease was a better sell if he put it in the context of a mutual need.

"Sounds like a good problem to have," Holly said half-laughing to herself.

"In a way yes, but people are rumbling about it," Rulon said telling her only half the truth.

"How could I possibly help you with that?"

"You could lease me the lot you have on the south side of your building; the one closest to the doughboy shop. If I could erect a sign that said it was overflow parking for Ellie's, that would help out a great deal."

"And how does that solve my problem?"

"Lease payments," smiled Rulon.

"Well, maybe this does sound interesting. How about we have some lunch and discuss it."

"That sounds like a fine idea," Rulon smiled back.

Holly signaled the bored waitress over and they both ordered lunch. They talked some more about the lease terms and by the time they had finished lunch they had a deal that was satisfactory to them both.

Holly was excited. With the influx of cash, she would be able to take out advertising in the local paper. She might even be able to afford some radio spots. She was wondering how costly those might be.

Rulon was happy about the lease. Because Holly was a bit desperate, he paid substantially less than he had anticipated. The town fathers should be happy that he was making an effort about the parking issue. Rulon was confident that they might leave him alone for a while as he sought a more permanent solution with his own lots next to his shop. If he got those, and he was hoping that Bill would get back to him quickly, he would have a surplus of parking and maybe he could dump the lease after a time.

The waitress put the bill on the table for the two lunches. Holly snapped it up immediately. "Lunch is on me."

"Well, thank you Holly. By the way, lunch was quite tasty. The food here is as good as I have heard."

"Thank you, Rulon. I'll take that as a genuine compliment."

"It is genuine," Rulon smiled at least he had mostly told her the truth.

Chapter 12: Thunder Rolls

Donna Reis sat quietly next to Jim Falmer at the city council meeting. The meetings were held in the beautifully restored city hall chamber. Despite its beauty, it was designed for a time when the city was much smaller and the attendance at such meetings was sparse.

The normal attendance at the meetings on a regular basis was hardly robust, but this night was certainly an exception. Jim and Donna had hit the phones and an abundant portion of the Carousel Foundation membership had made an appearance. They all knew that if the condo/marina project became a reality, their dream of installing a carousel at Cohassett Beach was certainly in jeopardy, if not dead altogether. They had all worked hard and long fundraising and carving horses, they were not about to let it all go to waste because of some developer's deep pockets.

The city council was assembled on the stage and was rapidly progressing through its regular agenda. Most items appeared on the agenda every month and were mostly procedural in nature and passed unanimously by voice vote. There was, however, a portion of the meeting reserved for public comment on non-agenda items at the end of the meeting and that is what Donna was waiting for. The city council members kept gazing out into the audience wondering what was of such interest to draw so many taxpayers to the meeting.

Most people were reclined in the auditorium seats contemplating the ornate ceiling that had been constructed over 160 years before. The ceiling depicted the solar system as it was known at that time. The outer planets had not yet been discovered. Most of the minds of the people in the auditorium were orbiting in those vacant spaces and paying little attention to the mundane proceedings.

The chairman banged his gavel. "I see we have a few people signed up to speak on non-agenda items this evening. Due to the lateness of the hour, we will limit comments to five-minutes for each person. The first name on the list is Jim Falmer," the chairman looked up, "Mr. Falmer."

Jim Falmer was a well-known businessman in the district and was politically active. He had held office in the past but had not run in several years. The chair looked directly at him when he called his name knowing that Jim Falmer did not speak on trivial matters. At this late hour, the chair was unnerved that Jim Falmer's name was on the list of speakers. Oh well, they would all know shortly what this was all about.

Jim made his way to the podium in front of the council, adjusted the microphone, and began; "Mr. Chairman, members of the city council, fellow residents..."

"Mr. Falmer," the chairman interrupted. "Could you state your name and address for the record." This was a frequently used tactic that unnerved most public speakers, but Jim showed no such nervousness.

"Of course, Mr. Chairman." Jim stated his name and address and continued like he had not been interrupted at all. "A matter of grave concern, which will soon be a matter of concern to you all when it is made public, has come to my attention." Everyone in the hall now sat more erect in their seats. Their contemplation of the cosmos had ended, and this was the moment they had been waiting for.

"A local real estate group is attempting to construct a condominium and marina project at Cohassett Beach. The effort has been underway for some time and would mean the destruction of the present community center, the taking of city beach property, and the dredging and removal of docks used by local shell fishermen." Jim Falmer paused and many of the city councilmen looked at one another knowing that a can of worms had just been opened and the odor would soon permeate the room and by tomorrow, the rest of the city.

It is common practice that the local paper sent a reporter, usually the lead reporter who was also the publisher, to city council meetings. The following edition of the paper contained an article summarizing the proceedings. The usually bored reporter, smelling a story in the making, snapped Jim's picture as he spoke and began scribbling hastily on his notepad.

"I find it unforgivable that this body would allow such a project to be permitted in the area. It has not so much as been discussed at a city council meeting and it is my understanding that the project is in the process of obtaining the city permits necessary to begin construction. Ladies and gentlemen; the first shovel of this massive, destructive project is about to go into the ground and this body has been mute on the matter."

It is also common practice that citizens are allowed to voice their grievances at the city council meetings. It is an unwritten rule that city councilmen sit stone faced during the comment session and not respond to the person at the podium. Several of the council members were now squirming in their seats. Joe Coleman, a council member sitting stage right, was texting on his phone and looked up when his name was called.

"Mr. Coleman," Joe Falmer loudly said into the microphone, "May I ask whom you are texting. Could it be you are sending a message to Governor Phillips, the head of the marina project, who supported you in the last election? That would be an ethics violation. We could subpoena your phone records to find out."

"Mr. Falmer. That is surely enough," stated the chairman as he banged his gavel, "Your five minutes are up. The next name on the list is Donna Reis." Jim Falmer quietly stepped away from the microphone. The Foundation had plenty of speakers listed to get their message across without violating any rules. He had lit the fire. Donna would now stir the pot.

Donna stepped to the podium and quietly gave her name and address. "I am the chair of the Carousel Foundation. We have been diligently working on carving horses for a new carousel to be installed at Cohassett Beach. We recently have a line on a carousel mechanism which we soon hope to purchase." There was a smattering of applause from the audience.

"The foundation has implored this body to allow us to install the carousel on city land at the beach," Donna continued. "We have been consistently refused. And now we hear that more land will be developed for commercial use depriving the citizens of this city access to dock space and the beach." Here Donna paused and stared at Joe Coleman. "Mr. Coleman. Am I boring you?"

Joe Coleman had once again begun texting on his phone. He was holding it below the table thinking no one could see. Unbeknownst to him there was no skirt on the table, and everyone could see, including Donna Reis who had the closest view. Mr. Coleman now made the grievous error of responding to a speaker at the podium.

"No, Ms. Reis. You are not boring me, and I am genuinely concerned about what you are saying. Please continue."

"Do you think that the city council should hear this matter and approve it before it is permitted to continue, Mr. Coleman?"

"Err...well...all matters that happen in this city should be approved by this body."

"And that's what I thought, too, Mr. Coleman. Yet, this body has not considered this huge project and it has not been deliberated in a public forum. What do you think we should do about that?"

Joe Coleman was now stuck between the proverbial rock and an extremely hard place. His fellow council members were glaring at him for speaking up at all. Yet, he had to answer the question. The crowd was restless and had been sitting for a long time. Some began to stand and were gesturing and yelling. The chairman banged his gavel to restore order.

When the crowd quieted and took their seats, Joe Coleman with sweat forming on his brow continued. "I do believe that this body should hear this matter. Due to the lateness of the hour, maybe we should table this," he said in a halting voice that almost sounded more like a question than a statement. He was looking at his fellow council members begging them for assistance with his eyes. He was drowning on his own and most of the members believed he deserved it for speaking up at all.

The audience continued their restlessness. The argument was going their way, but they knew there would be procedural efforts to squash this growing movement. Their voices began to amplify as it was evident that they wanted the council to do something. The council members were feeling it as well and the reporter was still scribbling notes on his pad. This would be in tomorrow's paper and some political face had to be saved.

"Order. Order," the chairman of the council shouted. "Point of order...there is no motion on the floor to be tabled and we are discussing a non-agenda item. We are out of order." There was silence in the room. The reporter was still writing.

"Mr. Chairman." It was Bill Healy, one of the senior members of the council asking for the floor. The chairman, feeling that this might be an out, recognized Bill Healy and granted him the floor.

"Mrs. Reis," Bill Healy began, "You are correct in raising this matter to the council. We should discuss it, but this is not the proper time. Mr. Coleman, if you would want to put your proposal in the form of a motion, I would second this matter for discussion and inclusion on next month's agenda."

"The chairman breathed a sigh of relief, "Mr. Coleman?"

"I move that we include the matter of the condo and marina development in Cohassett Beach for discussion on next month's agenda," said Mr. Coleman.

"I second the motion," said Mr. Healy.

"All in favor; signify by saying 'Aye'"

"Aye," as heard all around the table with a great deal of relief.

"The motion is approved. Will that satisfy you Mrs. Reis?"

"Thank you, gentlemen. We'll see you next month," said Donna with a satisfied smile. She turned to the crowd and raised her fists in victory. The crowd burst into applause and the meeting was hastily adjourned.

There was much back slapping and high fiving as the audience filed out of the auditorium. There were many cries of,

"See you next month," and "There's no way they're getting away with this."

Rulon sat quietly in the back of the auditorium watching the festivities unfold. Elias glanced his way a time or two and Rulon nodded. He could see a curl in the corner of Elias's lips. He let Donna and Jim revel in their moment and quietly got up from his seat and made his way out of the council chambers.

The reporter from the local paper elbowed his way through the crowd to interview Jim Falmer and Donna Reis along with others. The article in tomorrow's paper would be longer and much more interesting than usual. The publisher/reporter could feel his paper's circulation increasing as he wrote.

Chapter 13: Milky Way Tonight

"What time are Tom and Leah picking us up?" Russ called from the bathroom.

"They said six," replied Sophia from the bedroom where she was getting dressed.

"That doesn't leave us a lot of time," he said coming up behind her and hugging her around the waist. His hand started moving northward and she stopped him. She was wearing nothing but her bra and panties; a matching set she had picked up at the mall while shopping with Leah, her teaching partner and best friend.

"Oh, no you don't mister," she said twisting to face him. "You're not ruining all of this." She put her finger to his lips as he leaned in to kiss her.

Russ loosened his grip and held her hands at arm's length looking her up and down and admiring what he saw. "But when do I get to deeply appreciate what I'm seeing? Are those new, too?"

"Yes, they are. If you buy me a nice dinner and behave, maybe I'll let you have your way later."

"Promise?"

"I can't wait...but I will," she said giving his genitals a little squeeze and she took her dress down hanging from the closet door. Russ stood there looking forlorn.

"Chin up, bucko. Just think how much fun you'll have getting me out of this later," she said admiring herself in the full-length mirror. "Now, get dressed before they show up."

Leah and Tom seldom got to go out on a date. With two small children, it was a rarity. Leah was a bundle of energy and Sophia and Russ had doubled with them before. Russ and Tom got along so it was a good match all around.

Tonight, they were going to the Cohassett Beach Café. Tom and Leah only had a few hours while her mother watched the children. They didn't want to waste time riding to a faraway place for dinner. The café would provide a nice atmosphere at a moderate price for a comfortable dinner and conversation. Russ and Sophia having tried it for breakfast had recommended it.

Leah and Tom were on time. Russ saw them from the condo balcony and he and Sophia went down to meet them. Tom drove the short distance to the café. There was a decent crowd at the café and the first parking lot was tight, so Tom went to the lot beyond the restaurant. As he went to turn in, he noticed the sign 'Reserved for Ellie's Doughboy Shop' and went around the block and back to the first lot they had bypassed.

"Will you look at that," Russ said, "Mr. Drego finally has more parking for the doughboy shop. I guess our talk did some good."

"What's that Russ?" asked Sophia.

"The Captain sent us to talk to Mr. Drego about some complaints from neighborhood residents. One of them was parking and I see he has acquired more. I love when a plan works."

"Better than the alternative," said Tom. "I wouldn't want to issue a bunch of parking tickets to the locals for parking on the street. That would really cause uproar!"

"You said it."

They found a spot in the café lot and made their way into the restaurant.

"Detective Russ and Sophia...welcome back," Holly greeted them at the door. "I have your reservation...four for dinner. Right this way." They followed Holly to their table, and she seated them and passed out menus. "And who are your friends?"

"This is Leah and Tom," Sophia answered. "Leah is my teaching partner at the school and Tom is a lawyer in the city."

"Welcome to the Cohassett Beach Café. We have some specials tonight which your server will tell you about. We are a little busy, so I'll talk to you later. Bye for now."

Their server, Lori, came over and recited the specials for dinner. Tom and Russ liked the steak special and ordered that. The girls ordered seafood. All of them ordered drinks. When the drinks arrived, all of them toasted to a night out. Leah was especially exuberant.

"Sophia, would you like to go to the ladies' room?" asked Leah.

"Yes, I'd like to before dinner. Talk among yourselves, boys."

"Nice outfit Miss Fleming," Leah said as they entered the Ladies room. "Planning on losing it a bit later?"

"Well, yes I most certainly do, but I wouldn't brag Leah, that slit up the side of your skirt is riding a bit high."

"It's meant to. If I want Tom to initiate the proceedings, I have to show that I'm interested. And the way things have been going lately with the kids being sick and all, I am *definitely* interested! Must be nice having the apartment to yourselves all the time?"

"Yes, that's right...sex, sex, and more sex. That's how it is about our place," Sophia answered sarcastically. "We might not have sick kids, but plenty gets in the way of our love life. Russ working some of those odd shifts and the endless papers to correct from school doesn't create a turned-on atmosphere."

"I know what you mean. Sometimes you really have to work it."

"Ok, girl," Sophia said. "Let's work the magic and let them think we have been seduced." The two women finished touching up their makeup and made their way back to the table.

"And what are you two boys talking about?" asked Leah.

"We were just talking about the drop in the stock market this week," said Tom.

Leah gave him a look...

"And how great you two girls look tonight. Maybe we should skip dinner," Tom recovered.

"No, honey. We'll eat dinner, but you better sharpen up your charm if you're looking to get lucky tonight," said Leah.

"Oh, I'm just wondering if you're ready for this," quipped Tom.

" Alright you two. Our food is here, and they don't have rooms in the back so let's cool it. Sophia promised that I could get inside her outfit later. Let's eat so I can get to that part," said Russ.

Sophia slapped his wrist and they enjoyed a pleasant dinner with relaxing conversation.

While they were talking over drinks, Rulon Drego and Donna Reis were seated at the table next to them. Rulon was out of Russ' view, so he did not notice them.

"And how did you enjoy your dinners?" Holly asked standing at the head of the table.

"It was great. That steak special was really something. Tom and I both had it," said Russ.

"And ladies…"

"Oh, the baked fish was terrific," answered Leah.

"We liked our dinners, too," Rulon leaned in to answer.

"Mr. Drego," said Russ. "I hadn't noticed you there my back was to you."

"We came in after you. But Holly, really…our meals were excellent."

"Well thank you all. It's great to have satisfied customers."

"Donna, I enjoyed your speech at the city council meeting the other night," said Holly.

"You were there? I didn't notice you."

"I had heard you were going to address the council and I was wondering what was up."

Introductions were made all around.

"It really was a great show Donna and Jim put on. It really got the council's attention. I think the council is genuinely concerned," Rulon said.

Russ turned his chair to join the conversation. "I read John Anderson's column in the paper this morning. You seem to have stirred up quite the hornet's nest, Donna."

"I don't know about that, but it seems we struck a nerve. The next council meeting should be remarkably interesting," Holly said.

"Well, we've got to get going," said Tom. "It was nice to meet you, Holly, Donna, Rulon. Good luck with the restaurant. We enjoyed it very much."

"Thanks for coming in. I hope we'll see you again," said Holly.

"Count on it. Although we don't get out too often. Thanks again."

The two couples made their way out into the parking lot.

"It really is a beautiful night, how about a short walk along the beach? We have a bit more time," said Tom.

"Trying to romanticize me lover boy?" said Leah taking his arm.

"You bet ya, sweetie," said Tom.

"Sounds good to us," Sophia said taking Russ's arm and they strolled toward the boardwalk. The night really was clear and warm as they walked down the hill and passed the doughboy shop on to the boardwalk. There was only a quarter moon and the stars shone brightly. They slowed their pace as they reached the boardwalk enjoying their evening stroll.

+++++++

"Rulon, do you think we really have a chance to kill this thing?" asked Donna as they made their way to the exit of the cafe. "They are a powerful group."

"They might be powerful, but you have public opinion on your side. Governor Phillips and his cohorts tried to pull a fast one on the council and they don't appreciate that. I know you will get your membership there again next month and this time you get to speak at the beginning of the meeting. It might be contentious, but politically they will have a hard time giving their blessing to the project."

"I hope you're right, Rulon. A lot is riding on this. We need land for the carousel, and this might be our last shot."

"Don't worry, Donna. I told you I would help you out," Rulon said softly patting her hand and touching her just a bit longer than necessary. "If this project goes down the tubes and you get that mechanism, there will be a carousel in Cohassett Beach in two years." Donna did not pull her hand away.

+++++++

"Frankie, we're on the wrong street. Didn't you plan this out?"

"Dave, I told you. We're going to go for the back side of the restaurant. This is the street we need to be on." Frankie turned the stolen relic into the side street and began looking between the houses gauging where the back of the café was.

"I'm still not sure this is right. I can't see anything through the trees."

"Pipe down Dave. We just need to park the car."

97

"Where did you get this car anyway? I wouldn't be caught dead in this thing in the daylight."

"Dave, just shut the fuck up."

Dave was in the passenger seat of an old AMC Gremlin. The seats were torn, the body was rusted, and the radio didn't work. They were slowly moving down the side street adjacent to Cohassett Beach Avenue. It was a dead-end street that ran behind the cafe and the doughboy shop.

"You could have at least stolen a car that had a radio that worked."

"Dave, I swear...one more word. Here...we'll park it here and walk."

"We could get closer if you parked back there."

"Dave..." Frankie said as he turned put a finger in Dave's face. "Get the box out of the back."

Dave lifted the back window with a loud squeak. Frankie just shook his head. Dave went to shut the window..." Leave it open," Frankie whispered through his teeth. Sometimes Dave just got on his nerves.

The two made their way through the dark back yard of a three-story apartment building. Approaching the back fence, they were directly behind the Cohassett Beach Café. Frankie slapped Dave on the shoulder and pointed at the café. Frankie peered over the rotting cedar fence. There were a few pickets missing from the fence which made it easier to see the position of the dumpsters on the other side. The dumpster covers were open to make it easier for the help to throw the garbage and cardboard boxes into the bins. That was a stroke of luck.

"Dave…Dave…get the fuck over here," Frankie whispered. "Open the box." Frankie fumbled in the box finally finding what he wanted. He loaded a cartridge into the flare gun and aimed over the fence and into the dumpster. He pulled the trigger…whoosh! The flare gun fired, and the flare exploded into the dumpster. Frankie covered his eyes against the unexpected bright flash. Dave fell scattering the contents of the box.

The dumpster burst into flames. Frankie picked up Dave, the box, and what contents he could find. "Let's get out of here!" Frankie said.

Dave was laughing hysterically at Frankie. "Do you think that was loud enough?"

"Shut the fuck up, Dave." The boys made their way toward the car before anyone could see them.

They scrambled back to the Gremlin and made their way through the back streets away from the now flaming dumpster. Rulon would be pleased.

+++++++

The couples made their way along the boardwalk. The stars were luminous in the dark sky. They strolled in silence, hand in hand. At the end of the boardwalk they stood in silence watching the Milky Way, the men caressing the women from behind…they continued their silence as they admired the night sky.

Russ nuzzled Sophia's neck and she leaned back into him. "I'll give you several minutes to stop that," she whispered. Russ was encouraged.

Leah turned to Tom and pulled him down into a deep, passionate kiss which they held far longer than they intended.

Leah found herself breathing deeply as Tom's hands roamed over her. "I think you better take me home," she whispered, "Or we'll get arrested by the officer over there."

"I think the officer over there is not really paying attention to what we are doing. He seems to be starting his own fire," Tom said.

The couples broke their embrace as they heard fire trucks and sirens approaching down Cohassett Beach Avenue. They looked up to see a glow in the sky coming from behind them in the direction of the Cohassett Beach Café.

"Let's see what's going on," said Russ and they walked from the beach toward the café.

There were several fire trucks on the scene and the parking lot was an array of patrons, fire trucks, hoses, and flashing red lights as they arrived. Water was spraying from the hoses on a dumpster at the rear of the restaurant. It had been burning brightly when the couples approached, but the flames were quickly knocked down and there was an abundance of smoke, ash, and steam floating above them.

Holly, the owner, was in a flurry of activity and the fire captain was trying to calm her down. There was no real damage, but the fire had unnerved her, and she seemed terribly upset. Russ approached the fire captain.

"Is everything alright, Captain?"

"Oh, Detective...how you doing? Yes, we got here before anything spread and the fire was contained within the dumpster. There is no real damage. There might be some ash on the cars in the lot, but that's about it."

"That's good. Thanks Captain. We just finished dinner here and were having a walk on the beach when we heard the sirens. I'm happy that everything's alright." Russ returned to the group. "Everything is good and there is no damage. We can get the car out as soon as they move the trucks."

Rulon and Donna came out of the crowd and stood by Holly who was now seated on a chair in the parking lot. "Are you okay, Holly?" Rulon asked.

"I'm okay, Rulon. It's just the dumpster and there is no other damage. It just shook me up, that's all."

"Everything will be back to normal in a few minutes. The firemen seem to be packing up now."

"I hope it didn't upset the dinner crowd too much. Many of the patrons had started their cars and were leaving the parking lot. It's just one more thing gone wrong. The carousel ghosts must be angry with me."

Chapter 14: Sittin' on the Dock of the Bay

Donna Reis and Jim Falmer's speech to the Warwick City Council did ignite a firestorm in the city over the condo/marina project. Cohassett Beach residents and indeed the rest of the city could speak of nothing else. John Anderson's writings in the twice weekly local newspaper kept the story alive. Mr. Anderson attempted to collect interviews from the city council members, the mayor, former Governor Phillips, the state Department of Environmental Management, and anyone he could think of that might have had prior knowledge of the project. The matter did not leave the front page leading up to the next month's City Council meeting.

Speculation in the local restaurants and coffee shops was fierce. Just about every politician in office, with Governor Phillips as the primary target, was burned in effigy in every voter's mind. With the election less than two months away, the prospects for present office holders to retain their present positions was gravely in doubt because everyone had been tried, convicted, and the present politicos sentenced to the election graveyard for what they must have known of the project. It was only the right thing to do and obvious to all.

The story opined on the editorial pages and "factualized" on the front page and would not be silenced. Most politicians denied prior knowledge and were, of course, appalled. Leading up to the city council meeting the issue had become toxic with everyone denying that they had even considered supporting the project. Nary had a voter believed one word from the defense.

Donna gathered her membership and planned a filibuster at the city council meeting that would be akin to the parting of the Red Sea. The council members steeled themselves and were ready for the long night ahead.

The council members filed on to the stage and took their places behind their name placards at the table facing the robust audience that filled the city council chamber. The members had first met in executive session as was their habit and now settled in for the public session of the meeting.

The chairman banged his gavel. "The meeting will please come to order. Everyone please take your seats." He let a few minutes pass for everyone to get settled. He spied the appropriate players in the audience and made eye contact with Donna Reis and Jim Falmer. There was a group seated down front and to the right that neither Donna nor Jim was familiar with. They were a group of well-dressed men and women some of whom were in military uniform. Everyone assumed it might be for a presentation or an award of some sort. The committee preceded with their usual consent agenda and the group readied for battle when the flag went up.

"Next up is our usual public speaking session on agenda matters. I see we have several people signed up for that this evening," stated the chairman. "But if there is no objection from other committee members, I would like to delay the public speaking portion for just a bit so that we can hear from Dr. William Wangfort and his team from the Army Corp of Engineers...Dr. Wangfort." The audience grew restless. "Rest easy...no votes will be taken before you have an opportunity to speak," he said looking directly at Jim Falmer and Donna Reis.

Several of the well-dressed group to the right side of the audience moved into position. There were projectors and large screens set up. These were turned on and the lights dimmed. Dr. Wangfort and one of the uniformed men moved to the podium.

"Thank you, Mr. Chairman. I am Dr. William Wangfort with the Army Corp of Engineers and this is Major Kevin Steig, chief project officer for this study. We would like to present to you this evening our conclusions from our study of Cohassett Beach and our plan to rectify what we believe to be a serious situation."

Donna and Jim looked at each other and their membership. Everyone gave a shrug...no one knew what was going on. John Anderson, reporter, and publisher of the Warwick Times snapped a picture of the men at the podium and sat in his usual chair off to the side.

Dr. Wangfort and Major Steig explained with charts and graphs their extensive three-year study of the Cohassett Beach area. They spoke of mean high tides and storm damage. Beach erosion was deemed serious and its effect on the bay water was deemed catastrophic.

"In short," said Major Steig, "Something must be done, and it must be done soon." He then went on to outline a plan to rebuild the beach, install new rock jetties, and construct a new stone wall to protect the city park. "It goes without saying that all of this will be undertaken by the Army Corp of Engineers at no cost to the city or the taxpayers of Warwick."

Major Steig continued, "This is what we envision the completed project will look like with the beach reconstruction, the stone jetties, and the new stone wall." The Major's assistant showed a slide of a beautifully re-constructed beach area. The audience oo'd ah'd and then outright applauded.

When the applause died down, the Major continued. "This project will begin as soon as possible, and no dredging or other beach construction is possible during the two years it will take to complete the project."

Dr. Wangfort took the podium once again. "The detrimental effects caused to the fishery by the beach erosion and poor tidal flow must be corrected. If allowed to continue, the bay will be devoid of life within ten years. As a byproduct of saving this fishery, the city will end up with a beautiful and environmentally sound beach front. Thank you for your attention. Are there any questions?"

"Yes, Councilman Coleman," said the chairman.

"Doctor and Major you stated that the project would begin as soon as possible. Does that mean this fall season?"

"We would think that getting the proper equipment, materials, and permits in place would take until the fall. The heaviest part of the construction project would take place over the winter. The beach could be used next season if all goes well. The last portion would be the construction of the seawall and cleanup of the area in the second year."

"Thank you, Doctor. Anyone else? Councilman Fraiser."

"Major you stated that no other projects could take place during the time of beach reconstruction. How large an area does that entail?"

"Libby. Would you put that second slide up, please," Major Steig asked his assistant. The Major walked over to the projection screen. "We would need this area, (he indicated the ball fields) for staging equipment and supplies and we would be working along the beachfront and old seawall extending one hundred feet out into the water in all directions. Construction outside of those areas along Cohassett Beach Avenue would not be affected."

"Thank you, Major. Anyone else?" No hands were raised, and the report was accepted by a voice vote of the council.

"Now we move to the public comment section of our meeting. Mrs. Reis," said the Chairman.

Donna moved to the microphone. "Mr. Chairman and members of the council. I know that it is irregular to answer questions from the floor, but does what we just heard from the Army Corp of Engineers mean that the condo/marina project planned for Cohassett Beach cannot begin for at least two years?"

"You are correct Mrs. Reis. The council members do not respond to questions from the floor, but if you will allow me some latitude, I'm sure you will have your answer." He looked left and right at the other council members and they all nodded their assent. "Mr. Coleman, I believe it was you who raised the issue so I will allow you to make the motion."

"Thank you, Mr. Chairman. I move that the planned Cohasset Beach Condo/Marina permits before the council tonight be rejected at this time due to the work by the Army Corp of Engineers." The motion was seconded by many.

"All in favor signify by saying Aye." There was a chorus of Aye's.

"All opposed, Nay?" There was not a sound until a few beats later the room burst into applause and cheering. It took a good five minutes to bring the council chamber back under control. Most of the crowd had left when the council returned to its normal business. There was no further public speaking portion of the meeting that night.

Outside the council chambers, there was a good deal of back slapping and congratulations. John Anderson interviewed many members of the Carousel Foundation including Donna Reis and Jim Falmer. The article would take all the space above the top fold in the next day's paper. Below the fold would be the drawing for the new beach jetties and the seawall.

On page two of the Warwick Times the next day was an interview with Governor Phillips. With a quote, *"Due to the construction planned for Cohassett Beach by the Army Corp of Engineers, we have abandoned plans for a Condo/Marina project there in favor of another location across the bay."*

Chapter 15: Nothing Changes

"Good afternoon, Governor Phillips," Rulon said speaking into his office telephone. Rulon was positively giddy from the results of the latest City Council meeting. He tried to contain his excitement as he spoke with the Governor.

"Good afternoon, Mr. Drego. What can I do for you?"

"Governor, I would like to discuss a business proposition with you. Do you have any time for me this afternoon?"

"Of course, Rulon. Why don't we meet for lunch? Say 1:00 at Sam's Inn?"

"That would be great, Governor. I'll meet you there."

Rulon arrived about five after one and joined Governor Phillips at a corner table.

"Good afternoon, Governor."

"You're late," the former governor looked up from his study of the menu. The Governor was not actually upset with Rulon but looking to regain the upper hand. He was not really upset over the loss of the condo/marina project in Cohassett Beach either, except for the lost hours of work. The new location was proving grander than the Cohassett Beach project and would make as much money and provide as much satisfaction.

"Couldn't be helped," Rulon said not exactly being truthful. It could have been helped, if he had left on time, but he saw no harm in letting the Governor stew for a few minutes. Maybe it would be good for his humility index.

"Let's order. I have another meeting at two." They ordered lunch. The governor ordered a martini with his. Rulon ordered coffee.

Phillips sipped his martini when it arrived and over the rim of the glass said, "And what can I do for you, Rulon?"

"It's not what you can do for me governor, but what I can do for you."

"And what's that?" the Governor asked with a smile.

"You seem to own a piece of land in Cohassett Beach that is of little or no value to you and your partners."

"It would have been a lot more value if that group of engineers from the feds hadn't got their gander up to save the flounder in the bay or some such nonsense?"

"I think you and I both know, Governor, that; engineers aside, the project had hit a political wall and was never going to happen. Just reading the Warwick Times over the last few weeks would have told you that."

"You might be right about that, but we'll never know. Will we? Meanwhile we have moved on to another project across the bay that will probably prove more profitable, but I'm sure that is of little concern to you."

"You're right. I don't much care about your new project, but I do wish you well with it. I have other interests."

"Meanwhile, about the land I no longer have use for..."

"I'd like to take it off your hands, Governor. It would solve a parking problem for me and unload something you can't use right now anyway."

"We might be able to work something out." There was some talk about property rights, deeds, and price. By the end of lunch, there was a handshake agreement and both men were satisfied.

"Thanks for meeting with me Governor. We can let our realtors and lawyers work out the details."

"You're welcome, Rulon. I've got to go." With that the Governor rose and buttoned his jacket. "Oh, and by the way, you're buying lunch."

+++++++

Back in his office Rulon was feeling very satisfied with himself. He had acquired land across the street from the doughboy shop from the Governor. He had told Webster Phillips that he needed it for parking, but he had other plans. He had been mulling over a sit-down restaurant for years. He had built up his brand, but parking and the land to put it on was always a problem. Maybe the Army Corp of Engineers had done him a great big favor.

Within two years the beach would be completely rebuilt. There would be a new city park and parking area. Stone jetties would replace the crumbling wooden affairs which would draw even more people to the beach. People have to eat, and his doughboy shop and take-out seafood restaurant stood ready to serve them. If he had his way, his sit-down restaurant would be ready for the masses in less than a year.

If he indeed wanted to get a permit for a sit-down restaurant, he would need even more parking. The city fathers would never allow another restaurant to open with the present, available parking. He really didn't need the competition from the café to muddle the waters and divide the customers either. It was time to turn up the heat.

Rulon picked up the phone and dialed. It was answered on the second ring, "Do you know who this is?"

"Yup."

"Meet me behind the convenience store in ten minutes."

"See you there." The phone went silent in Rulon's hand.

"I'll be back in about a half-hour, Jill," he told his secretary as he passed her desk. Rulon made his way to his car, this time leaving the top up. He drove to the convenience store about a half-mile up the road and pulled into the back-dirt lot. Frankie was waiting with his window down. Rulon pulled alongside.

"Hey Frankie," he said as he handed an envelope across the space between the two cars.

"Hey, boss. Thanks," Frankie said reaching out and taking the envelope.

"Nice job with the dumpster the other night."

"Thanks. It did go up pretty quick," Frankie said laughing.

"Yes. It was a good show. I need to change some things about the café. Despite your effort so far, the business there is still doing okay. I would like it to...er...begin to change that."

"How's that?"

"Do you still have your motorcycle?"

"Sure. That's my pride and joy. Keep it shined up and running like a kitten...preserved it in a friend's garage during my stay in the state pen."

"Yeah. Yeah. You still hang around with that group of riders?"

"You mean the motorcycle club? Of course."

"Why don't you and your friends start going to the café. They could use the business if you know what I mean."

"We used to go there when it was a biker bar, but it ain't exactly our kind of place anymore."

"Why don't you make it your kind of place, again?"

"I don't know, boss. The boys don't exactly go for the lace curtains and stuff."

"There is more than enough cash in that envelope for free meals for all of your friends. Maybe you could take the lace curtains down and rearrange the décor more to your liking while you're there."

"Huh?"

In a sterner voice Rulon said, "Maybe you could bust up the place while you're there."

"Oh. Yeah. Maybe we could do that after dinner."

"Now you got it, Einstein." Rulon spun the tires a bit on the gravel as he left the lot.

Instead of going directly back to his office, he went out to the avenue and stopped by his realtor's office. Rulon didn't bother stopping at the secretary's desk, but rather breezed by saying, "Is he in?" The secretary tried to block Rulon's path, but she was too slow in her high heels. The secretary was stammering some sort of apology by the time Rulon was sitting in a visitor's chair in Bill's office.

"Rulon. Great to see you. I was just going to call you." Bill waved to his secretary that it was alright.

"Cut the bullshit, Bill. What do you hear about those two lots next to my doughboy shop?"

"Funny you should stop in today. I'm told they just went on the market."

"And you were going to call me when?"

"I've been busy, Rulon."

"More bullshit, Bill. Talk to me."

"Since the condo/marina project got cancelled last week, the owners want to sell. They don't see any upside to holding on to the property any longer. Maybe it was best that you waited."

"Those bloodsucking bastards wanted to open up a rival doughboy-clam cake shack next to me for years. They just didn't pull the trigger and they were waiting for the condo people to either buy their land or bring in more customers. Snap up those two lots for me and low-ball the offer. They are stuck with them and I'll bet they really want to unload. Make it happen, Bill. Today!"

With that Rulon stood and left the office like he was responding to a fire. The tires again squealed on the pavement as he made his way back to his office.

"Mr. Drego," his secretary said as he entered. "Governor Phillips left a message for you. He wants you to call him as soon as you came back"

"Thanks, Jill. I'll do that right away." Rulon went into his office and dialed the number on the slip his secretary had given him.

"Hello again, Governor. How can I help you?"

"The land is yours. I'm having the papers drawn up. We can sign them tomorrow. Stop by my office around two."

"Thank you, Governor. Nice doing business with you. Have a nice day." Rulon hung up the phone and did a little victory dance in his chair punching the air several times through the open door he said, "Jill, get me Elias Fraiser on the phone."

When the phone buzzed, Rulon picked it up.

"Councilman Fraiser on one," said Jill.

"Thanks, Jill. Would you close the office door please?" Rulon pushed the button for line one.

"Elias, how are you?"

"I'm, feeling much better. Thanks. How are you?"

"I'm fucking fabulous!" answered Rulon.

"Well I'm good, Rulon, but what you have sounds a whole lot better."

"Things are really working out, Councilman. First, the condo/marina project gets cancelled."

"Well, that wasn't all our doing. It was actually a stroke of luck. The Army Corp of Engineers concluded their study and wanted to report to the council. We weren't even sure what they were going to say."

"You could not have coached them any better. Our political noses are clean, and we didn't have to use our ace in the hole."

"I think the project would have had no chance with the shit-storm that erupted after the last council meeting. And the Carousel Foundation didn't even get to present their case," noted Elias.

"You got that right, but the Governor and his friends will never find out what we did because the Army Corp did it for us."

"Ain't it grand, Rulon. Sometimes you are just a lucky bastard. But you're feeling better than just that. What else happened?"

"Two things. First, I bought that land from the Governor."

"The condo/marina land?"

"That would be the parcel."

"You opportunistic bastard, Rulon. You must have got a great price."

"That I did. And second, the two lots adjacent to the doughboy shop came on the market and I'm going to snatch them up, too."

"You have wanted those two parcels for years. Good for you. With all of that, you are positively giddy."

"You're going to be giddy, too. You know those plans I've had for the sit-down restaurant…"

"Yes."

"How would you, and your construction company, like to start building that as soon as possible so that I can open in the spring?"

"That's a tall order, but I think we can get it done. Do you want it next to the doughboy shop?"

"No. No. Across the street so that it can have a view over the new park and the sea wall. The Corp will be using the ball fields, but our project is smaller than the condo/marina project and is outside the Corp's construction area."

"That sounds marvelous. I'll pick up those drawings and start the permit applications tomorrow."

"The sooner the better, Elias. The sooner the better."

Chapter 16: Smoke on the Water

Rulon was feeling on top of the world. With his newly acquired land and plans to build; he was finally going to realize his dream of owning the beach. Governor Phillips was out of the picture with the rest of his cronies and Rulon was controlling the action in his part of the world. He had slaved over that fry-o-lator for years and now it was his time to shine.

Rulon took a glass from his side drawer and poured himself two-fingers of bourbon. He had stopped at the liquor store and bought some Wolford Reserve. No more cheap stuff for him. He examined the caramel liquid glistening with sunlight from his office window overlooking the bay making the amber bourbon look like gold. He took a sip and enjoyed the taste of the fine liquor as he swallowed slowly. He didn't hear the door open behind him.

"Enjoying an afternoon delight, Rulon?" a female voice said as Rulon swung around in his chair to see Donna Reis standing before him.

"Donna! "Care to join me? You're early for our meeting."

"Don't mind if I do," Donna said removing her light jacket and putting it over the back of a chair.

Rulon took out another glass and poured some for Donna. He got up and walked the glass over to her. She put the glass to her lips and took a sip.

"Oh, you've graduated to the good stuff. You must be getting up in the world."

"Oh, yes. Things are looking up. And if they're looking up for me, they're looking up for you."

Rulon circled her chair and noticed that she was displaying her rather nice-looking tanned legs. He had not often seen them because she frequently wore jeans. Today, Donna was wearing a blouse and skirt which fit her well with low heels. She was quite a nice package when she dressed the part. Rulon sat back in his chair and sipped his drink.

"We make a pretty good team; you and me," Rulon said.

"That we do," said Donna and she took another sip. Her glass was almost empty. Rulon held out the bottle and she offered her glass. He poured her more. He also refreshed his own drink.

"So, you got what you wanted with the condo/marina project," Donna stated.

"And so, did you."

"That's true. We didn't even have to roll out the big guns."

"Well, I don't know about that," Rulon said. "You fired a pretty big gun at the council meeting last month and you were ready to drop a bomb at the meeting last week. With John Anderson's help in the Times, it seems you had the council eating out of your hand."

"I wouldn't have known to do that without the information you so handily provided."

Rulon gave her a smile. "I do what I can," he said holding out his hands, palms up and shrugging his shoulders.

"Sure, you do; when your interests are at the heart of the matter."

"We all have our business considerations."

"And what are yours lately?"

"I can tell you that I have bought the land across the street from Governor Phillips."

"Is that for me and my carousel?"

"I did say that I would get you the land that you needed. I'm not sure that is the right place for it, but it could be. Let's see how things develop."

"What are you looking to develop?" Donna asked. Her voice seemed to have become huskier as she drank. Was the whispered suggestiveness in her voice real or was that just his imagination? Rulon wondered as he poured Donna a bit more bourbon.

"Would you like to move over to the couch?" he asked. Might as well find out what her intentions were.

"That does look rather comfortable over there. Why not?" Donna moved to the couch and slipped off her shoes. She tucked one leg under her and afforded Rulon an even better view of her legs. Rulon put the bottle down and joined her on the couch, laying his arm across the back.

"All this business talk makes me tired. What else can we talk about?"

"How about we talk about your legs? How do you keep them so evenly tanned?"

"Oh that," she said running her hands along her one outstretched leg. "Just a lot of time on the beach." Did her skirt move higher through that movement? She made no move to pull it back down.

"Do you tan all over?"

"Do you mean what I think you mean?"

121

"Is your tan as even as it seems?"

"Oh, you naughty boy. I bet you would like to see." She unbuttoned the top button of her blouse and pulled it back a bit. "What do you think? All the way or not?" Rulon gazed at Donna's cleavage. He saw no white lines. Damn, she did look good.

Donna emptied her glass and placed it on the side table. Her motion exposed more of her cleavage and when she turned back, she gave him a smile. She patted his hand on the back of the couch. "Oh my...my. Am I torturing you? I feel the same way about the land for my carousel."

"Maybe we can come to some agreement?" Rulon said moving closer.

"Yes, I think we can," Donna said leaning her head back and allowing Rulon to brush her lips with his. She felt his hand inside her blouse pushing her bra aside and brushing her breast. She caught her breath and Rulon covered her mouth with his.

There was no further discussion of business or land as he removed her blouse and skirt. She helped with the rest as Rulon removed his own clothing. Donna lay back on the couch and she wrapped herself around him as she welcomed Rulon's advance and he fell into her embrace.

When they were finished and their breathing returned to a more sedate level Rulon said, "We should get dressed, Elias will be here soon. Hope I didn't wrinkle your blouse."

"It'll be fine. I just hope my excitement can subside and I don't give away our earlier activities. Where's your bathroom?"

"Behind that door," he said indicating a door in the corner of his office. "I'm still pretty revved up, too. I hope Elias doesn't stay too long."

They had just finished dressing and tidying up when Elias came in.

"Elias. Right on time. How are you?" Donna greeted the councilman.

"I hope I didn't keep you waiting."

"No. No," Donna said smiling at Rulon. "I just got here myself. Would you like to join us in a drink?"

"Don't mind if I do. It has been a long day." Rulon got another glass and poured Elias a shot of bourbon. "Nice, the good stuff." Elias took a pull of his drink and sat back on the couch. Rulon sat in an armchair and Donna sat on the other end of the couch. "Pretty comfortable couch, Rulon."

"Yes, it is," added Donna and gave Rulon a sideward glance. Rulon could hardly contain his own smile.

"I thought we might get together to solidify future plans," Rulon began. "With the governor and his group out of the picture, what might Cohassett Beach look like in five years?"

"I might be able to help there," said Elias. "I managed to abscond with a print of the Army Corp of Engineers plan for the beach reconstruction and what it will look like when completed." He unrolled the print and placed it on the coffee table.

"Look," said Donna. "They are showing the community center, the reconstructed ball fields and basketball courts, the apartment building, Ellie's Doughboy Shop, and the Cohassett Beach Café. The rest is empty lots."

"You both know that I purchased the lot across the street from the Governor and, what you don't know is I have a bid on the two lots next to the doughboy shop," said Rulon. "That purchase should be completed next week."

"So, you've solved your parking problem," said Elias.

"I would say so," stated Rulon. "I would finally like to build my sit-down restaurant. I've wanted to do that for years."

"And where would you put that?" asked Donna.

"The best place with the best view is across the street on the Governor's old land. It has the best sight lines to the water."

"I see that, but I thought that was for the Carousel," said Donna with a bit of an edge in her voice.

"Don't get upset now Donna," said Rulon in a calm voice. "What if we planned the carousel for its original location at the top of the hill?"

"But that land belongs to the Cohassett Café?" questioned Donna.

"I don't think that establishment will be in business in two years...maybe not even next season," said Rulon.

"What are you planning?" Donna asked implying that Rulon may be up to no good.

Rulon patted her hand. "Don't jump to conclusions, Donna. I know from Holly that the Café is having financial problems. That's why she leased the parking lot to me. I think that money is keeping her afloat, but I don't need her parking anymore because once I pave these two lots," he indicated the lots next to the doughboy shop, "I won't need to lease the lot from Holly."

" That could be brilliant, but that café building is an eyesore."

"Not if it isn't there. If the parking extends from the doughboy shop up to the carousel," Rulon pointed out the area on the map, "it can service the entire avenue. That, with the new beach parking constructed by the Army Corp of Engineers will be all the parking we could need. No more harassment from the city fathers, the doughboy shop, a sit down restaurant, and the carousel with a community center with ball fields and basketball courts...the beach will be the playground that it was meant to be."

"You're a genius, Rulon."

"Thank you, Elias."

"It's a brave plan. I like it," beamed Donna.

"Well, that's it for me. Got to get home to the Mrs. Donna, Rulon...I'll get on those permits first thing next week," and with that Councilman Fraiser finished his drink, set down his glass, and closed the door behind him as he left.

There was no pretense between Donna and Rulon. As soon as the door closed, clothes went flying and flesh was exposed and greedily embraced.

Chapter 17: Born to be Wild

"Did you have any problems with the permits for the restaurants, Elias?" Rulon was standing with Elias outside the doughboy shop on the sidewalk looking over the work being done on the new parking lots.

"Not at all, Rulon. Once the city planners saw how much parking you had, they couldn't turn you down. We're a go for the whole project."

"How long for these two lots to be paved and striped?" asked Rulon.

"They will be ready for Saturday if the weather holds. We finish leveling today. We start paving tomorrow. Give it a couple of days to cure and the striping and you're good to go."

Elias and Rulon had moved up the hill on the sidewalk as they were talking. The large graders had done their work and were being loaded on to flatbeds for transport. Smaller units were finishing up the leveling work. It had been two weeks since he had acquired the land and already, they were making great progress.

"When can we start on the restaurant?" Rulon asked.

"As soon as we're done here, I'll send some of the equipment across the street to level that parcel. We'll need some fill, but we could start on the utilities in a week…again…the weather."

"Okay, Elias. That all sounds good. I think I better handle this." Holly was coming down the sidewalk at a brisk pace. She was making a beeline for Rulon and she had fire in her eyes.

"What the hell is this, Rulon? You're making your own parking lot now and you cancel the lease with me. I thought we had a deal. You send me this letter…You couldn't tell me to my face!"

"We did have a deal, Holly, a monthly lease. With these two lots, I no longer need yours so, I cancelled the lease as of the end of the month."

There were tears in her eyes. "I'm operating barely in the black at the café and this was keeping me above water."

"I told you that the restaurant business is a long haul. You have to give it time."

"I can't go on much longer." She was breaking down and was very frustrated. "What am I supposed to do? The winter months are coming, and business will wither to nothing. I don't know if I can make it to the spring."

"Is there anything I can do to help?"

"I think you've done enough already." With that she reversed her step and trod back up the hill toward the café. She crumpled the letter Rulon had sent, tore it to shreds, and tossed it all over the sidewalk.

"I think she's pissed," Elias observed.

"Oh, yeah. She's pissed."

+++++++

Frankie and Dave road their bikes down Cohassett Beach Avenue leaving a wretchedly loud, thunderous noise in their wake. They were decked out in their colors with black bandanas wrapped on their heads, black leather jackets, and leather chaps, with heavy leather heeled boots.

They gunned their bikes as they pulled into the café parking lot. Frankie parked his bike along the back fence where no cars were parked. Dave pulled in next to him.

The two strode into the café and took seats at the bar. The few patrons eyed them suspiciously. Holly was in the back room when they were seated. Frankie ordered them two beers.

A short time later, another motorcycle was heard pulling into the lot. Johnnie "Thumbs" came in dressed similarly to Dave and Frankie. Johnnie's girl was in leather shorts and a midriff top. They took a seat at a table and asked for menus.

Dennis "McEvil" came in a short time later with his girl Lisa displaying her wares spilling from her tight leathers for all to see. By this time, Holly had come out of the back and became concerned with the looks of things.

"Can I help you?" Holly asked Dennis and Lisa as they surveyed the room for a table.

"We would like to have dinna. Is that ok wich you?"

"I don't want any trouble."

"No trouble from us. Hey, boys," Dennis asked loudly. "We're just takin our broads out to dinna at a fancy place. OK?"

"Okay but look...I don't want any trouble. I'll serve you dinner, but please don't..."

"Don't what pretty lady?" Dennis was standing close to Holly and it made her nervous. "You're gonna serve us dinna...I should be frekin' honored or somethin'?

"Dennis let's just sit and have dinna," Lisa said smacking her gum loudly.

"Alright. Alright."

Donna showed them to their table. Waitresses took orders and the motorcycle boys and girls seemed to enjoy their dinner. Johnnie walked over to the bar where Frankie and Dave were finishing up their plates. Without warning, a plate flew from Frankie's hand and crashed into the liquor bottles at the back of the bar.

"Hey, knock that off," warned the bartender. Frankie leaped over the bar and began beating the bartender. A patron tried to come to his aid, but Johnnie jumped in. Before anyone knew it, plates were flying, curtains were ripped off the windows, and the few patrons remaining were headed for the door. Holly was dialing 911 as soon as Frankie went over the bar.

Two cruisers responded immediately and restored some semblance of order. Russ and Carl, working the late Saturday shift, responded a few minutes later.

Carl and Russ went over to Holly who was sitting at a table crying. "Holly, its Detective Russ Deever. This is my partner, Carl Resendez. What happened here?"

"First...those two...came in and...sat at the bar.... then that guy and his girl came in.... then those two. I warned them...I didn't want any trouble." She broke down and couldn't go on for a few minutes. "Then...once they ate...that one threw a plate at the back of the bar and jumped the bartender. Then.... he..." she indicted a customer being treated by the EMT's... "tried to help and really all hell broke loose after that."

"Alright Sergeant," Russ said talking to the lead patrol cop. "Let's get some statements from everyone. Then we'll decide who we're going to run in." The patrolmen went about their business and Russ and Carl went over to talk to Frankie who had the makings of a shiner and a split lip.

"Hey, don't I get no medical help?" asked Frankie.

"In due time, tough guy. Bartender got in some good shots, didn't he?"

"He ain't so tough. Look at him."

"What are you guys doing here?" asked Russ.

"We used to come here all the time. Rulon told me it was open again, so I thought we'd try it again."

"How do you know Mr. Drego, Frankie?"

"How do you know my name?"

"I arrested you a while back at Big Ern's. I'm hurt you don't remember me."

"Oh, yeah. I remember now."

"So, how do you know Drego?"

"We went to high school together."

"So, Mr. Drego sent you here?"

"Well, not in so many words, but yeah."

"Thanks." Russ turned, "Sergeant, you can haul this one down to the station. We've made his acquaintance before. He's probably violating his parole. You can arrest the rest of the participants in this melee."

Russ and Carl went over to speak with Holly. "How are you holding up?" Carl asked.

"Oh, I'm okay, but would you just look at this place. I don't know if I can recover from this."

Russ and Carl looked around. The place really was a mess. Most of the liquor on the bar was destroyed. There were overturned tables and broken chairs. Decorations had been ripped from the walls. Most of the curtains had been torn. It had been a cute place and now it was a wreck.

"Won't the insurance cover the damage?" Russ asked.

"Oh, sure. But it will take days to clean up and the deductible will kill you. I just don't know if I have the energy to start over," Holly sobbed.

"We're sorry. We'll try to get to the bottom of this," Carl said, and they left Holly among the rubble of her ruined restaurant.

Chapter 18: Out Go the Lights

"Come on Carl. Let's go for a walk." Carl and Russ made their way down the hill from the cafe toward the doughboy shop.

"There must be something we can do to help Holly out," Carl said as they walked.

"Oh, I think if we do our jobs, we can find out what is really going on here. I smell a rat. I also think we're headed for his nest right now," Russ said in a voice that was becoming angrier the more he spoke. "Hey look," Russ said pointing at the freshly asphalted parking lots. "It looks like Rulon has at least taken care of his parking problem."

There was the usual line outside and down the sidewalk waiting to put in an order at Ellie's Doughboy Shop window. Every evening there was a line, but on the weekends the line stretched down the street. Carl noticed the trash cans were overflowing with refuse.

The detectives bypassed the crowd and flashed their badges at the inside service window and asked for Mr. Drego. They were directed down the hall to his office.

They entered the office area. There was no secretary at the desk in the outer office and the door was closed to the inner office which indicated it belonged to Rulon Drego by the gold leaf lettering. They hesitated at the door and listened. There were noises coming from inside Rulon's office. There was heavy breathing and the movement of furniture. It sounded like someone was resisting an attack.

Russ looked back at Carl. Carl nodded. "Someone could be being hurt behind that door," Carl said.

"I think so, too," said Russ. Russ knocked twice on the door and walked in with Carl right behind.

"Excuse me, Rulon. Would you like to introduce me to your friend? And we need to talk." Before them were Rulon and Donna in a significant stage of undress laying half on the couch and half on the floor. The couple looked up with looks of shock on their faces. Donna let out a scream that came out more like a squeak. Then, they began to cover themselves.

"We'll give you a minute." Russ and Carl backed out into the outer office closing the door quietly behind them and trying to stifle their laughter as they waited.

"You think we should have stayed?" asked Carl.

"She does seem like a looker, but that is definitely not his wife," Russ whispered.

"Secretary?" asked Carl softly.

"I don't think so. I've seen his secretary. She's a blond."

"Then who was that?"

"Someone he obviously gets along with very, very well. It's Donna Reis, Chair of the Carousel Foundation. They were having dinner at the Café when Sophia and I were there. Things are beginning to make a lot more sense."

A few minutes later, Donna came out of the inner office wearing more clothes than before, but still looking disheveled.

"Have a nice evening, Ma'am," Carl said politely.

Donna gave them both a look that could have struck them both dead. The detectives went back into Rulon's office.

Rulon was tucking in his shirt. "What the fuck's with you guys. Can't you knock?"

"Ugh...we did. Maybe you didn't hear us. Getting some extra work done at the office?" asked Russ.

"Don't fuck around with me. What do you want?"

"There is a problem up the street."

"What the hell does that have to do with me?"

"It seems you know the leader of the problem. Remember Frankie?"

"Frankie who? I don't know any Frankie."

"Frankie that you went to high school with...talked to recently...and told him the café was open again? Or at least that's what he says."

"So what? I was here in my office. I was obviously busy. I didn't do anything."

"Well, you sure were busy doing something when we came in. I think I've seen your wife in your commercials. Her name is Ellie, right? And that," Russ said pointing to the office door, "wasn't her."

"Just a friendly relationship; doesn't mean anything," said Rulon.

"I think your wife might see it quite a bit differently. Anyway, it seems that the café is all busted up and Holly has the impressions that you might be behind it. Looking at who's involved, I tend to think she may be right."

"You got nothing on me. You want to haul me in for an illicit affair, you got me there, but you got nothing else. A bunch of bikers bust up a café and it's supposed to be my fault?"

"I didn't mention anything about any bikers," Carl said. He and Russ stared at Rulon who seemed to have nothing more to say.

"I think you better come with us, Mr. Drego," Russ said.

"Am I under arrest?"

"We can make it that way, if you want or you can follow us in your own car."

"And besides, your trash can is overflowing on to the sidewalk" Carl said.

Rulon picked up the keys on his desk and followed them out pulling up his zipper as they walked.

Chapter 19: Every Picture Tells a Story, Don't It?

"Captain, you got a minute?" Russ and Carl were standing at Captain Marep's door.

"This isn't going to turn into a fucking circus, is it?"

"Ahh…more like a merry-go-round.; a carousel to be exact," Carl said with a smile that quickly disappeared with a look from the Captain.

"Oh, you two; like clowns in the big top. Is this gonna get my ass burned by the mayor? You got all my interrogation rooms filled up, it's the end of the shift, and I would like to go home sometime soon. What?"

"Were getting the dandiest, most convoluted story. We got Rulon Drego, owner of Ellie's Doughboy Shop, having err…intimate relations with Donna Reis, the leader of the Carousel Foundation."

"So, the guy is getting a piece of ass on the side. Good for him."

"Well, it's not just that. Mr. Drego just bought the land that Governor Phillips was going to build that condo/marina development that got rejected by the Army Corp of Engineers work on Cohassett Beach and he intends to put a sit-down restaurant on it. Mr. Drego also bought two lots adjacent to the Doughboy shop and he's making those into parking lots for the Doughboy Shop and his new restaurant."

"Sounds like he's buying up land to expand his businesses and getting a piece of ass on the side," said the Captain. "Get to the point, Detective. I've got a promise myself if I don't get home too late." He checked his watch. "And it's getting to be too late."

"According to Holly Richards, the owner of the Cohassett Beach Café, Rulon is trying to put her out of business. First, it was a dumpster fire, then, he cancelled his parking lot contract with her, and now he's sent a biker gang to bust up the place. Did a rather good job of it, too."

Carl added, "The biker gang is mostly a bunch of misfits that we busted last year for transporting drugs in the Big Ern caper."

"In short Captain," Russ said. "I think we can pin Rulon for manipulating this whole mess. And as for his piece of ass on the side, she is trying to firm up, so to speak, the land for the Carousel her Foundation needs at Cohassett Beach. She said that Mr. Drego promised it to her."

"So, you have found quite the can of worms and you have spun quite a tale. Why are you telling me all this now? Just put it in your report, book the one's that committed a crime, and let's all go home." The Captain checked his watch. "Shit it's too late now anyway. Lori won't even be up now when I get home. What else?"

"To put a cap on this, we would like to go and talk to Governor Phillips. He might be miffed about losing the land and the project and tell us something about Mr. Drego. What do you think?"

"You know that is a fine piece of crystal you are dealing with there." The Captain sat and thought for a moment. "Go and talk to him but bring your white gloves...your very best pair...and treat Governor Phillips gently or you both might end up with singe burns on your ass."

"Thanks, Captain. We'll handle with care."

"Yeah, Yeah. That's what you always say and then I end up in front of the Chief holding my ass in my hands. Now get out of here."

+++++++

On Monday, Russ called Governor Phillips' office and made an appointment for the next afternoon. He and Carl had some other cases they were working on. They had a couple of leads, so they went out and did a couple of interviews concerning those.

One of the cases involved a complaint from a citizen in the Cohassett Beach area. The complaint outlined a problem with cars chewing up her lawn and parking on her property. It was minor, but they thought they would stop by and see if anything would pop up seeing as how it related to Rulon Drego and the parking dilemma.

Carl found the address. There was an older man with a rake and shovel attempting to resurrect his front lawn. The house was not new, but well-kept with fresh paint and trimmed bushes. It appeared that several cars had made deep tracks in the muddy ground of the front yard and grass sidewalk. Once the lawn dried out, deep ruts were left, and the lawn was ruined.

Russ and Carl parked their car a bit up the street and walked toward the man working the rake. "Good morning, Sir. I'm Detective Deever and this is my partner Detective Resendez." The two displayed their badges to the older gentleman and he examined them with squinting eyes.

"What can I do for you officers err...detectives?"

"We received the complaint about the ruts in your lawn and we're here to follow up," said Carl.

"That would be my wife. I told her it was a waste of time. What did she expect; the public works department to come by and fix it? That's what I told her. You're not here to help me out, are you?"

"Aahh, no sir. We're here to find out what happened."

"Two cars parked on my lawn going to that blasted doughboy shop. That Drego doesn't have enough parking. They leave trash all over the place. I clean it up all the time."

"Sorry about that sir, but Mr. Drego is putting in more parking so that should help out and he has added more trash cans."

"About time! I damn near sold out to that real estate outfit that wanted to build those condominiums at the beach. They were a mighty hard sell, but I held out and they finally backed off."

"That project has been cancelled, sir," said Russ.

"Damn glad to hear it. That would have been an eyesore and where would I have docked my clam boat?"

"Guido, who the hell are those men?" An older woman, presumably Guido's wife, was hanging out of the front door yelling for the whole neighborhood to hear with a broom in her hands.

"It's about your complaint about the lawn, Irene. They're asking me some questions."

"You tell them about that son of a bitch Rulon Drego," she was still yelling, "with all of his trash and the cars on our lawn?"

"Yes, ma'am," Russ answered trying to bring the volume of the conversation down. "Your husband was very helpful."

"You tell them Guido. You tell them about that son of a bitch." With that she slammed the door and went back in the house.

"My wife gets a bit excited about all the trash and the cars. She even tried to chase a couple of people parking their cars off our property with her broom. It was quite the sight."

"Yes, sir; I'm sure it was," said Carl. "You said that someone came here to try and get you to sell your home?"

"That's right. Been here almost fifty years. Tried to run us off. I was having nothing of it. Would have sic'd Irene on 'em if they hadn't left. She would have gladly taken a piece out of their hide."

"I'm happy it didn't get that drastic," Carl chuckled.

"Don't laugh Sonny. You two seem nice so I kept her in the house," Guido grinned.

"Did anyone come back after that to pressure you?" asked Russ.

"That dandy Rulon Drego came by and harassed me about the complaint Irene made. Tried to push us around, you know...he didn't put his hands on me or nothin', but he was trying to scare us. I let Irene out of the house, and he left real quick and didn't come back." He plastered a wide grin on his face once again.

Russ and Carl couldn't help but smile a bit as they imagined Irene and her broom confronting Rulon Drego. They could imagine Irene chasing Rulon back into that shinny convertible and peppering him with that broom.

"Guido, do you know that the city has free black dirt at the recycle center?"

"Nope," said Guido. The boys explained where the recycle center was and Guido thanked them and said he would be heading there to fill in the ruts. "See, you boys did come to help. I'll be taking my old Ford over to that there recycle place and pick up some dirt. I can stop at Benny's on the way and pick up some grass seed."

"Serve and protect, it's what we do but Guido, but the Benny's store closed last year."

"You don't say. Where am I going to buy my grass seed now?" Guido said sadly shaking his head.

Chapter 20: No More Cloudy Days

"Warwick Police; Detective, Deever?" Russ answered his telephone.

"This is Lisa from Governor Phillips office."

"What can I do for you, Lisa?" asked Russ.

"I am calling to confirm your appointment with the Governor today at 2:00," Lisa said in an efficient voice with just the right amount of professional sweetness.

"Yes, that's right. Is there a problem?"

"No, detective. There is no problem except the Governor spends most of his time at his new development, Hill and Harbor these days. Would it be very much trouble if you came here for the appointment?"

"No, that would be fine," Russ answered.

"We'll expect you at ten then." She gave him directions on where to park. "There is quite a bit of construction activity so be careful of that."

"Thank you. Two it is then. Goodbye Lisa."

"Goodbye Detective."

Carl gave him a look that said, 'What?"

"We're still on for two with the Governor except that now we're meeting him at his new Hill and Harbor development," Russ explained.

"I've been wanting to get a look at that new place. Joelle and I went to a wedding there a few years ago and it was nice then. I hear he is really sprucing the place up."

"That's what the papers said. Did you see the drawings?" asked Russ.

"Yeah...golf course, banquet hall, condos, marina...the works. Sounds like some upscale living. Real gentrified just like the plans were for Cohassett Beach, but it doesn't seem so out of place across the bay."

"It does seem better suited to the new location and now it has a golf course included. You and I won't be moving in there any time soon."

"Well at least we got invited. We better get going," Carl said.

Russ and Carl made their way out of the office and heard the Captain bellow, "Russ...Carl." They stopped and peered into the Captain Marep's office. "Don't fuck it up," the Captain said looking stern.

"No sir," they both answered and continued out to the station parking lot.

"Does he really think we're going to screw this up?" asked Carl.

"Nah. He's just making sure we don't."

There was furious construction in progress at the new Hill and Harbor Luxury Resort when Russ and Carl pulled their car into the lot and parked as directed. The golf course was being revamped, the second condo building was under construction, and according to Carl the banquet facility had been completely renovated. Half the docks in the marina had been replaced and work was in progress on the remaining old docks.

"They saw the Governor standing with a group outside pointing in several directions and seemingly directing a multitude of operations at once. When he finished speaking, the workers all dispersed heading in several directions. The Governor saw them approaching, waved, and walked down to meet them.

"Thank you for meeting me here Detectives," and he shook each of their hands and introductions were completed. "Why don't you come up to my office? We can talk there. It's a bit quieter."

They made their way through the entrance to the banquet facility to a corner office overlooking the golf course and marina. The office had surely been selected for the best possible view.

"This is going to be a fabulous facility, Governor," Carl said.

"It already is and it's only going to get better. Those dumb bastards in Cohassett Beach could have had all of this and more, but they fought me to the end."

"I thought the Army Corp of Engineers put a hold on the construction."

"Oh, that's what everybody thinks, but the project was dead long before that," said the Governor. "I'm sorry. I'm prattling on. What is it you boys wanted?"

"Well, it's all about that Governor," said Russ. "We're trying to piece together what is going on in Cohassett Beach. We have parts of the story and our suspicions about the rest, but we just can't pin down Rulon Drego's part in all of this."

"Rulon Drego is a snake. Everyone thinks he is just a shrewd businessman. He is an agitator and a spineless son of a bitch."

"We have heard others refer to him as such, but what makes you say it?" asked Carl.

"Okay...from the beginning," started the Governor. First, my partners and I proposed the condo/marina project for Cohassett Beach. We tried to keep it quiet so we could buy up the land we needed."

"We hear you put some pressure on people to sell out?" asked Russ.

"Well, I suppose we did, but that happens when you are trying to put together a large parcel from many small ones. Some people just don't want to sell."

"Maybe they just want to hold on to their homes?" said Carl.

"Shit. In the end we were offering them double what their homes were worth, but that's all water under the bridge. Drego and that slithering councilman Fraiser conspired with that bitch Donna Reis to use the Carousel Foundation to kill the project. They didn't have the balls to do it themselves, the cowards, so they had a woman do it for them. Of course, in the end the Army Corp of Engineers killed it anyway and well...that was that."

"I suppose you could say that Drego was just protecting his interests in the beach, but your dislike seems to go a bit deeper," said Russ.

"And so, it does," continued the Governor. "Rulon Drego bought the land for the condos from me after the project collapsed saying he wanted it for parking. Now that rat is building a restaurant on it. If I knew he wanted it for that, I would have charged him a lot more."

"Again…crafty business…"

The Governor cut him off, "And then he bought the two lots next to his own place for parking and is trying to drive that woman out of the café because he wants that land, too. He wants more parking and land for the Carousel that he promised that wench, Donna Reis."

"Err…it seems you might be assuming quite a bit there, Governor," said Carl.

"I assume nothing. You two check into it further and you'll find everything I'm telling you is the truth. That guy is a venomous snake and he is driving everyone out of Cohassett Beach so that he can have it all for himself. I don't believe for one second that he ever intends to give that land to the Carousel Foundation. He only keeps telling Donna Reis that so that she'll keep satisfying his sex drive."

"Well…you sure have given us more information than we ever suspected and filled in a few holes in the story we had. What you have told us ties many of our suspicions together, but not a lot of it is criminal, just underhanded. Maybe we can make something of this if we just keep digging."

"Keep digging detectives and I'm sure Drego is behind several illegal actions. He covers his tracks well."

"Thank you for your time, Governor."

The Governor rose from his chair and shook hands with each of the detectives. "You get that bastard…he deserves whatever he gets."

"Err...thanks again," Russ said. Carl and Russ walked back to their car dodging the frenzied construction activity.

"You get the feeling that the Governor doesn't like our buddy Rulon," said Carl.

"Ya think?"

Chapter 21: The Division Bell

Cases come and go for detectives on a city police force. Some are major and some are minor, but all of them are important and serious to the people involved. Russ and Carl flowed with the workload every day, but there comes a time in a case that you turn it over to the attorneys and the investigation is completed. Then, the case is closed as far as the police are concerned.

Some cases stay in sharp focus due to media attention, but most quickly fade into memory. Many cases languish in investigation until the moment when they are to appear in the courts. Such was the way of charges against Frankie, Dave, and Rulon, et al. The lawyers delayed proceedings in the hope of discovering some loophole or the police making an error with evidence allowing them to get their clients off on some technicality before they ever had to appear in court.

Attorneys are famous for this tactic. They say that they are busy preparing their client's case when really, they are racking up billable hours. As they accumulate ever higher bills, the clever attorneys hope that in their frequent exchanges among the agencies will cause a procedural error that will tie a judge's hands and either get their client off or get the charges reduced.

Thus, is the ploy of defense attorneys. Those charged with crimes love them for it, though they hate the billable hours. The police and the prosecution just dislike criminal attorneys from the start and can't believe they defend the scumbags. But alas the cases drag on.

So languished the cases involving those in the Cohassett Beach matters. Of course, those wronged saw no satisfaction in all of this. Their losses still existed. Their problems caused by the allegedly guilty parties still had to be dealt with. Truthfully, the guilty held all the cards as everyone tried to protect their rights while the wronged just wallowed in the mire of their troubled hearts and minds and the mess created by those that had wronged them.

So, it came that in the early spring Russ and Carl stopped by the Cohassett Beach Café to see how Holly was doing and to let her know that the case was still alive and would come before the courts in a short time. They decided to meet their wives for lunch at the Café. Sophia had the day off from school. She and Joelle were already seated when Russ and Carl arrived. Sophia saw them walk in and waved them over. Russ and Carl made their way to the table for four and sat.

The place had been neatened up since the bikers had destroyed it but didn't show off that cuteness as it once had. Store bought curtains now hung in the windows replacing the ones Holly had made. The liquor bottles on the bar had diminished in number and the bartender and the waitress were now one in the same person, at least for lunch. The staff reductions made it clear that the restaurant was not doing as well as it once had.

Holly came over to see them. "Welcome back. I see you have brought friends," she said handing out the menus.

"This is my partner, Carl and his wife Joelle."

"Now I remember you Carl. It was a bit hectic last time I saw you," Holly said as she turned toward Joelle, "and Joelle. I love your hair."

"Thank you," said Joelle. Everyone knew that Joelle was stunning. She was humble about it, but she glowed with that healthful look that some people just have. She didn't work at it;

she was just born with it. To listen to Carl talk, she only shared it with him. "I go to Hugo's salon in Coventry. I owe it all to him," Joelle said.

"And Sophia, looking lovely as always. How are the kids treating you at school?" Holly asked.

"They let me think that I'm in charge most of the time. So, it has been good. I'm looking forward to spring break though."

A young woman came to the table and passed out four glasses of water and a basket of bread. "Here's Lori. She'll be your waitress and bartender today. No doubt she will take good care of you. The lunch specials are inside your menus." With that Holly moved off to greet other diners.

"Would anyone like a drink besides the water?" Lori asked.

"We're on duty, but you girls go ahead," Carl said.

The girls ordered a glass of wine each and Carl and Russ got an iced tea. When Lori returned with the drinks, Sophia asked, "Seems a little depressed in here. Is everything all right with Holly?"

Lori distributed the drinks and took a deep breath. She looked around and spotted Holly far across the room. "I've been here since we opened, and it's never been this bad. Since the brawl, the customers have stopped coming and we might not make it through to the summer season. I work lunch alone every day and it is hardly worth it. Holly is getting more depressed all the time and I worry about her."

"Maybe we can cheer her up a bit before we leave. The case is coming up in court soon."

"That's great. Those bastards should get what they deserve, but Holly may never recoup what she has lost. It is sad to watch. What do you guys want for lunch?" Lori asked.

They ordered lunch and in a short time, Lori efficiently brought their food. "She's good. She remembered what everyone ordered," Sophia took note. "We should leave her a good tip."

"She even brought all of condiments we needed, too. Didn't have to ask for another thing," observed Joelle.

"No wonder she can work alone. She is a good waitress," said Carl.

"Good help is hard to find. Too bad this place might go under. She might be looking for another job soon," said Russ.

"Maybe she can get a job at the new restaurant across the street. I was looking as we came in. It looks like it's almost completed," said Joelle.

"The sign said the grand opening was in three weeks. Maybe we should try it," said Sophia.

"After dealing with that guy Drego, I don't know if I can," said Russ.

"Me either," said Carl. "He is a dark character."

"Can I get you anything else?" it was Lori clearing up the table.

"How long do you think the Café will last? Business will surely pick up as the weather improves?" said Carl.

"That's usually true, but once Drego opens his new restaurant; who knows?" said Lori sadly.

"Maybe you could work there?"

"Never. That man is the devil. I'll never work for him," Lori stated talking through her teeth. It was evident that she did not like Drego.

Sophia and Russ talked to Holly for a while telling her about the case while Carl and Joelle went to the bathroom. After a few minutes, Russ and Sophia started looking for Carl and Joelle, but they didn't seem to be coming along. Russ was getting nervous as they were due to call in soon.

"So, you think this maybe it for you in the restaurant business?" asked Sophia.

"This has taken all my energy and it seems I'm pushing against the tide. It's just too tough. If I can get out and maybe break even by selling all the equipment; I'd do it in a heartbeat," said Holly.

"That's too bad, Holly," said Russ still looking over his shoulder for Joelle and Carl, "I really like it here. I'll miss it."

"Thank you, Russ. I'd like to say I'll miss it too but...well, the people I'll miss, but the work and the hours; not so much," said Holly.

"Ah, here they are," said Sophia finally seeing Carl and Joelle emerge from the back of the restaurant. "What took you so long?"

Carl and Joelle filed by the group without making eye contact like they were trying to avoid recognition on a perp walk. Joelle was straightening her clothing and making a beeline for the car. Carl didn't look back either.

"What's with them?" asked Sophia. Russ just squeezed her hand and led her out of the restaurant. "Are they okay?"

"They are more than okay," Russ said giving Sophia a kiss. They went to their separate cars.

Russ got in the car and gave Carl a look. "What?" Carl asked.

"What you ask. What the hell were you doing?" Carl just smiled. "...oh, you dog. In the ladies' room?" asked Russ.

"No, the men's room. She surprised me. What was I supposed to do? She just came in and unbuttoned her blouse and then..."

"Enough. I don't need any more details," Russ said covering his ears. "Middle of the day! Really! And on duty, too!" And they both started laughing. They looked over to the other car and Joelle and Sophia were in stitches. Russ tooted the horn and waved to them as he drove from the parking lot.

Chapter 22: Sitting on Top of the World

Rulon Drego emerged from his offices at Ellie's Doughboy Shop into a bright, abnormally warm, early spring day. He took a deep breath of salty air and looked back at the shop from the sidewalk.

The little doughboy shop that he had bought 25 years before had become an icon in the Cohassett Beach area and in Rhode Island for that matter. In the last five years it had been completely rebuilt and now looked more like a restaurant than a doughboy shop. The paint was gleaming in the spring sunlight and the new sign and logo looked great.

The serving line was not too long today, but on the weekends, it frequently stretched down the sidewalk toward the beach. Everyone knew about Ellie's. He had made a lot of money, but he had worked hard. In the beginning, he toiled fifteen-hour days at the fry-o-lator with oily residue penetrating every pore of his body. He was happy he didn't have to do that anymore. Now he hired college kids in the summer and kept the best ones on through the winter season.

He turned and looked at his latest creation across the street, Ellie's Pier Restaurant. The colors, décor, and style of the buildings were a perfect match. Diners would soon be able to sit in comfort and be served fine seafood dishes as they overlooked the bay with sunset views and salty breezes. It would be grand, and it was all his.

He stepped into the street and heard the screeching of brakes as a car stopped short to keep from hitting him. He hadn't even noticed the car approaching. The driver shook his head and waved for Rulon to cross before proceeding to the beach parking lot. Rulon waved back as if apologizing for his carelessness.

Entering the front entrance of Ellie's Pier, he was greeted with workers putting the finishing touches on everything from moldings to paint. Fixtures were being hung and furniture was being assembled and placed in the dining room. Boxes of liquor were being unpacked as the bar was stocked and kegs of beer were being rolled in through the service entrance.

Entering the kitchen, he saw stainless steel everywhere; sinks, ranges, walk-in freezers...it was all top-of-the-line. "Mr. Rulon isn't it magnificent!" exclaimed his new head chef Federico. "This will be the finest kitchen anywhere. We will prepare the finest dishes and patrons will come from miles around." Federico embraced Rulon encircling him with his burly arms. Frederica's Italian accent and mannerisms were endearing, though overdone; after all he was born in Fall River, Massachusetts.

"Yes, Federico. It will be marvelous," Rulon said releasing himself from the big man's burly arms. "Together we will show the world what a fine restaurant should be. I love this kitchen," Rulon said patting Federico playfully on the cheek. "I must check on the progress with the rest of the work to be sure we are ready for next week." With that Rulon went out into the bar area and dining room to check with supervisors to be sure preparations were going as planned. He could hear Federico barking orders to workers in the kitchen.

When he was satisfied, Rulon stepped back out on to the street. He looked up the hill and looked at the Café. He sighed and took his first step to cross the street; looking both ways this time, towards a conversation he knew would be unpleasant.

The café building seemed to sag in sadness as compared with the new Ellie's Pier building. He could almost hear the business gasping as he approached. Holly was desperate and Rulon knew it. It was time to make her an offer to get her to finally give up the café. Only then would his plan be complete. He reached the café, put his hand on the doorknob and entered.

There were only a few customers in the restaurant. There were two men drinking at the bar and one couple eating lunch. He looked around and saw Holly sitting at the end of the bar. He approached her with a smile.

"Holly, it's nice to see you," Rulon said slipping on to the bar stool next to her. How have you been?" He noticed there were fewer bar stools. Some must have been broken in the melee. There were fewer tables and chairs, as well. The place had an atmosphere of a hospital room containing a terminal patient. You could almost hear the faint beep, beep, beep of the faint, failing heartbeat of the place.

"You can guess how I've been Rulon. Look around, I can't go on much longer like this and once you open Ellie's Pier… well, that will be it. This place will be dead."

"Sorry to hear that, Holly. I never meant to hurt you."

"Sure, Rulon. You always had my best interests at heart," Holly whispered sarcastically.

"Its business, Holly; just business."

"Yeah…just business," sighed Holly. They sat there for a few minutes and neither of them spoke. The silence mixed their emotions…Rulon's ecstasy about opening his new place which he was hiding with great effort and Holly's depression about closing hers which she was making no effort to hide at all. Those whirling emotions caused the turbulence in the room that was palpable to them both.

"Holly, maybe I can help."

"Oh, I think you may have helped enough already, Rulon."

"You said you wanted out of the restaurant business; didn't you?" asked Rulon.

"I did, but not by choice."

"How about if I buy you out?" There it was out. He wasn't sure how he was going to propose it to Holly, but there it was.

Holly just looked at Rulon. She really didn't have anything to say to that.

"I mean for a price and then you can step away from all this. It may be the best offer that you get."

"After you open the Pier, I don't think anyone will want this place. What did you have in mind and what would you do with it?" Holly asked.

They talked for a while and finally settled on a price that Holly thought was fair considering the circumstances and would allow her to walk away with not devastating damage to her credit, but yet a big dent to her bank account. She had tears in her eyes the whole time, but she realized that it was the best and maybe the only deal she was going to get.

Rulon inwardly smiled. He was getting exactly what he had wanted all along and now it would be all his. He gave Holly just what she needed to get out with an acceptable loss. He knew the land was worth more, but hey, it was just business. She was a nice lady, he thought, but she really didn't know much about business and even less about real estate.

Rulon never did answer her question about what he was going to do with it.

Chapter 23: Saturday Night's Alright

"What are you doing on your day off tomorrow, Carl?" Russ asked.

"Joelle has us slotted for a barbeque at her parents' house," Carl answered with a bit of a sigh.

Russ and Carl were pulling a second shift on a Saturday night. It had been quiet, and their paperwork was up to date. They were lounging at their desks in the squad room passing the time.

"Oh, that's right. Tomorrow is the big day," Russ said.

"Yep, Joelle's father, the one and only Big Ern is getting out of the federal pen. He's been a good boy, so they're letting him out early. He's lucky to get out at all. He got a fairly light sentence and a nice comfy cell at a country club penitentiary in New Jersey," said Carl.

"Do you suppose he's seen the error of his ways?" asked Russ.

"I don't think he'll be getting anywhere near drug trafficking in the near future. He's been released in my mother-in-law, Bunny's custody. I don't think he wants to violate that. After all the bull she's put up with, violating parole will seem like a cake walk if he violates Bunny one more time."

"How does Joelle feel about her Dad getting out?"

"She's a bit apprehensive as you might imagine. Big Ern put the family through a lot. They won't put up with him stepping out of line. Maybe Ern's brother Dino will let him work at the car dealership."

"Well, that's also part of his work release. He's wearing an ankle bracelet and the only two places he can be are the dealership and his home. He has to do that for a year. I know it will drive him crazy, but the alternative is back to the pen and he doesn't want that."

"I know going to your in-laws is not your favorite thing, but try to have a good time," said Russ. "And give Joelle my best."

"It'll be even better if Joelle takes me down to the pool house again," laughed Carl.

"You are a lucky man, Carl; a lucky man."

"Don't I know it."

"Deever, Resendez; you're up," came the voice of Captain Marep. "Reported altercation down at the new Ellie's Pier restaurant in Cohassett Beach. Units are responding; better get a move on."

"We're on our way," said Russ as he and Carl grabbed their sport coats from the back of their chairs and headed out.

When they arrived at Cohassett Beach there were three squad cars with their lights flashing, a fire truck, and a rescue squad in front of Ellie's Pier Restaurant. If there was a fight, there were sure enough people to control it; including the shift sergeant, additionally; someone must be hurt for the EMT's to be on the scene. They parked the unmarked detective car where they could and walked the rest of the way.

They located the shift sergeant. "What have you got Matt," Russ asked.

"From what I can gather, that lady over there," he pointed with his pencil at Holly Richards sitting with one of the patrolmen, "hit that man over there in the head with a wine bottle", he pointed at Rulon Drego who was holding a compress on his forehead soaked with blood flanked by a patrolman and being tended to by the EMT's. "And that woman over there" he pointed at Donna Reis sitting next to Holly, "punched Mr. Drego in the mouth." The bartender: he pointed again with his pencil, "called 911".

"How bad is Mr. Drego hurt?" Russ asked the EMT.

"He'll need a stitch or two, but he'll live. The bleeding is controlled for now."

"And the women; any injuries?"

"No sir. Just a bit shaken up." It was obvious that Holly was in a highly emotional state. She was crying and looked quite distraught. Donna Reis was sitting quietly.

"They're frekin' crazy. Those two bitches are nuts," Rulon declared in a loud voice for all to hear pointing at Donna Reis and Holly Richards.

"Easy Mr. Drego," said Carl. "Just tell us what happened."

"They came in here during our grand opening and came over to my table and made a scene; yelling and screaming at me about how I had cheated them both. Then Holly picked up the bottle of wine from the table and hit me with it. While I was stunned, the other bitch punched me in the mouth. I want to file charges."

"Sure, Mr. Drego. We're going to let the EMT's transport you to the hospital so that you can get medical care. This officer will follow to take your statement. We'll be in touch. Once you're medically stable, please come down to the station to fill out a formal complaint, if you're so inclined."

"You better believe it. I want them arrested," Rulon insisted.

"We'll handle things here. You just go and get treated. We'll talk later."

With that, the EMT's walked Rulon out to the waiting Rescue. Russ and Carl made their way over to where the ladies were sitting. They motioned for the officer to bring Donna Reis to another table out of earshot of Holly. Carl read Mrs. Reis her rights.

"Are you feeling alright, Ms. Reis?" Russ asked.

"Better than I have in a long time."

"Can you tell us what happened?"

"That bastard Drego called me and told me that he was buying the Cohassett Beach Café, but he had decided that he needed all the land for a parking lot and there was no room for the Carousel. That son-of-a-bitch had promised me that land. The Foundation was counting on it."

"And what happened here this evening?" asked Carl.

"I went to the Café and was sitting at the bar with Holly. She told me what Rulon had done to her. We had a couple of drinks and decided to come down here and confront him. The smug bastard just shrugged us off, so I punched him in the mouth."

"How many times?"

"Just once. Holly had already hit him with the bottle. He was pretty woozy."

"Ms. Reis, I'm afraid we'll have to place you under arrest and take you down to the station for processing. Do you understand?"

"Yes, I do. Can I have my husband meet me there?

"You can call him from the station," said the patrolman and he escorted Donna Reis to his patrol car.

Russ and Carl then made their way over to Holly Richards who was still shaking and crying. They informed her of her rights, and she nodded that she understood.

"Can you tell us what happened, Holly? Why did you come down here?" asked Russ.

"That rat-bastard Drego tried to buy me out for a song. It was insulting. I found out I could get much more for the café than he offered. He was stealing it from me after driving me out of business. He deserved what he got."

"And what happened when you came down here?" asked Carl.

"Donna and I were telling each other our sob stories and having a couple of drinks at the bar up at the café. Did you know Rulon was having sex with her?"

"Err...yes, we knew."

"Anyway, after a couple of drinks one thing led to another and we came down here to give him a piece of our minds. When we went to his table, he treated us like dirt. He didn't want to hear it and called us a couple of naïve broads."

"And..."

"And that's when I picked up the bottle from the table and hit him with it. He got a little groggy but was still being cocky with us and mouthing off, so Donna punched him."

"Just once?"

"One bottle; one punch…he went down after that."

Russ explained that Holly was also under arrest and gave the same instructions to the patrolman.

They talked with the bartender, and he verified the stories they had heard. The other officers had taken statements from other witnesses, so their work was done. The waiters and waitresses were cleaning up while the questioning was going on. Business was back to normal as the fire and police vehicles were departing.

On the way out Carl said, "Reckon Rulon got what he deserved."

"And you…an officer of the law," said Russ.

"I'm more about truth and justice," said Carl.

"And the American way," added Russ.

Chapter 24: Have a Nice Day

"Deever. Resendez," Captain Marep's all too familiar bellow came from his office.

Russ and Carl made their way to the Captain's door. "Yes, sir," Russ said sticking his head in. There was a man in a gray, well cut suit sitting in one of the Captain's visitors' chairs. He turned to look at them. Russ recognized him as one of the prosecuting attorneys that worked for the city. "Hello, counselor."

"Detective. This is your case; the Cohassett Beach thing?"

"Yes, it is. Is there something we can do for you?"

"Ahem...if I could get a word in edgewise in my own office...this is attorney Jim Cristo. These are Detectives Deever, whom it seems you already know, and Resendez his partner. The detectives have worked several aspects of this case and I'm sure they can fill you in."

"Nice to see you again, Russ; Detective Resendez," Jim Cristo said in the way of greeting.

"What would you like to know, Jim?" asked Russ.

"Ahem...feel free to use one of the interrogation rooms, gentlemen. I have a department to run," injected the Captain.

"Oh, right," said Jim. "Lead the way boys."

The three men made their way to one of the rooms used to question witnesses and suspects. They sat down. "Coffee anyone?" asked Carl.

"Don't mind if I do," said Jim.

"Get three, Carl. Thanks," said Russ. Russ and Jim got caught up with small talk while Carl fetched the coffee and then Jim said shaking Russ' hand, "Congratulations on passing the bar, Russ,"

"News sure does get around. I was trying to keep that quiet."

"When one enters the brotherhood, the brothers always know," said Jim taking a seat. "When can we expect you to come over to the dark side and start working as a prosecutor?"

"Not soon, Jim. I still have some work to do here."

"That may be, but the pay is a lot better and it's the same retirement system. You know we would welcome a former police detective to the city attorney's office with open arms. It would make a great liaison back to the police department for our office."

"Thanks for the glowing recommendation."

"If you ever need a letter for your resume, you know where to find me."

I'll remember that, Jim. And thanks."

Carl came into the room carrying three coffees and put one in front of each of them and took a seat at the table. "So, what do you want to know? Everything we know is in the file," said Carl.

"Well, yes, I read that, but I'm confused. There are a lot of players and what seems like a mountain of deception, lying, and cheating, but no big crimes. Mr. Drego is insistent on filing charges against Ms. Richards and Ms. Reis for assault and battery, but other than that it just seems like a lot of underhanded business dealings."

"I think you've about got it, Jim. Drego is a conniving sort that lied to Reis just to get in her pants and he misled Richards to get his hands on the Café. He duped Governor Phillips who has no love for him, and he is an ambitious letch when it comes to business, but he didn't really commit a crime other that being a slime ball," said Carl.

"So, the crux of the matter is Drego filing charges against the women for hitting him: one with a bottle and one with a fist. The women are half-justified in that he misled them both, but that doesn't get them off. I wonder if Mrs. Drego would be very delighted to hear of the affair between Rulon and Donna Reis," said Russ.

"I really don't want to prosecute these women, but with Drego filing charges, I don't have much choice. Maybe I could have a conference with opposing counsel, the women, and Drego. Then I could let Drego see what might become public during a trial if this goes to court."

"Maybe the parties will all be satisfied with what has transpired thus far and let it drop there. It's worth a shot," said Russ.

"Well, at least the girls thought so," said Carl.

+++++++

When Russ and Carl entered the court, the parties were already seated at their respective tables. Russ went up behind Jim Cristo and whispered, "So what happened at the conference?"

"Drego is adamant about pressing charges so we'll proceed with the hearing and see what happens."

"Should be interesting?"

"That it should."

Russ went back and sat next to Carl. Carl shrugged his shoulders and spread his palms. "Drego wants to go through with it. His wife must be a mouse," Russ told him.

"It is my experience that in these matters a mouse turns into a ferocious, biting rat when her husband cheats. Drego is playing with fire," Carl stated.

"All rise," the clerk announced. "Court is now in session; The Honorable Camille Francis presiding. Please be seated."

Russ looked at Carl, "He is screwed."

"The next case is Drego v. Richards and Reis Your Honor," the clerk announced.

"Are all parties present?" Judge Francis asked; not bothering to look up from the file she was perusing.

"Yes, Your Honor; Jim Cristo for the prosecution." Jim stood at the prosecution's table. Rulon started to get up then awkwardly sat back down.

"Your Honor; Kim Fargo for the defense," a woman with short black hair dressed in a business suit said standing at the defense table.

"He's double screwed," Carl whispered to Russ.

"To summarize the facts of the case, Your Honor," Jim Cristo began," Ms. Richards and Ms. Reis entered the premises of Ellie's Pier Restaurant on the night in question. They approached the table where Mr. Drego was seated and after a short conversation, Ms. Richards hit Mr. Drego in the head with an empty wine bottle and Ms. Reis punched him in the mouth."

Kim Fargo stood. "Additionally, your Honor, there are some circumstances we should discuss."

"Are you disputing the facts as described by the prosecution, Ms. Fargo?" asked the Judge.

"No, your Honor; but there are associated facts that the court should hear."

"I allow it for now but understand associated facts may not make it to trial."

"Yes, your Honor."

"Proceed."

Ms. Fargo began. "Mr. Drego has harassed Ms. Richards in her operation of the Cohassett Café. He even went so far as to send a biker gang to disrupt the business and err...rearrange the décor."

"That's a lie," Rulon stood and shouted. Jim Cristo was about to object, but Rulon beat him to it.

"Ms. Fargo. Please control your client. Mr. Drego, I'll have no further outbursts in my court. You will have your say," Judge Francis said all this while pointing her accusing finger at Rulon. Rulon sat back down without saying anything else. Judge Francis' finger moved with Rulon as if pushing him back into his seat.

"Do you have witnesses to substantiate your claim?" the Judge looked at Ms. Fargo.

We do your Honor."

"Then continue," said Judge Francis glaring at Rulon.

"Additionally, Mr. Drego promised land to Ms. Reis as president of the Cohassett Beach Carousel Foundation for the Cohassett Beach Carousel with some strings attached."

"Strings?" asked the Judge.

"Continuing intimate relations."

Rulon stood. Jim Cristo stood. The Judge glared and pointed her finger. Rulon slowly sat down.

"This is all getting very convoluted. It seems we have misdeeds on top of misdeeds ending in violence at Ellie's Pier."

"Oh, that won't be the end of it," a woman was standing in the middle of the court. She had styled, short, black hair, a pretty face, and nice clothes. Together they were a very presentable package. She had two small children: one holding each of her hands.

"Here we go," whispered Carl. "He's triple screwed."

"And who are you?" asked the Judge.

"I am Ellie; Mrs. Drego." The assembled crowd in the court room took in a collective breath and held it.

" Mrs. Drego, what do you wish to add?" the Judge finally said.

"I have been married to Mr. Drego, the alleged slime ball, for twenty years. We have worked to make Ellie's a success, but now he has smeared our name. I think you should throw the book at him."

"Mrs. Drego, he is the one bringing the charges. I can't send him to jail."

"You can either send him to jail or I will lock him up so tight that he will wish you had." With that Mrs. Drego sat down with her two children."

"Russ turned to Carl, "He's screwed either way."

Judge Francis continued. "I am a resident of Cohassett Beach and have watched these developments from afar. It seems there are more people we want to hear from before proceeding. I would like to see the two attorneys and their clients in my chambers for a conference." With that she banged her gavel and left the bench.

"I would love to be a fly on the wall in that conference," whispered Carl as they were making their way from the court.

Russ' phone vibrated and he checked the message. "You get your wish. The judge wants us in chambers."

The two attorneys stood before the judge's desk in her chambers. She took off her robe and sat behind the desk. She pointed at everyone else in the room. "Sit in the chairs back there," she pointed to chairs along the wall, "And speak when I ask you to." Everyone sat. The attorneys remained standing.

"Now; this misdemeanor has come before me and I smell a rat. In fact, I smell a pack of rodents so I'm going to get to the bottom of this. Then, decisions will have to be made. Am I clear?" Everyone nodded.

"Detectives," the judge said looking at Russ and Carl. They nodded. "Could you put together a short list of people who could offer testimony as to what the hell is going on here?"

"Yes, your honor," answered Russ.

"Then you do that. Then, meet with the two counselors here, get their input, and get that list to me pronto…like today."

"Yes, your Honor."

"Counselors; you will confer with the detectives to make sure that I am getting the whole picture. I don't want a whole lot of squabbling over the list. Understand?"

"Yes, your Honor," the attorneys both answered.

"You all go away because the court has other business today. Get that list to me and get those people in the courtroom tomorrow. We'll reconvene at ten. Don't be late. Now, go."

Judge Francis spoke as they all were leaving, Detective Deever."

Russ turned, "Yes, your Honor."

"May I see you a moment."

Russ went back in and stood before the judge's desk. She was also standing behind it. When everyone had left, she came out and extended her hand to Russ, "Welcome to the bar, counselor; well done."

Russ shook hands with Judge Francis, "Thank you your Honor."

+++++++

The attorneys and the detectives made their way to police headquarters. They worked for about an hour before finally settling on a list and an order of presentation to the judge.

"She is not going to like this," said Kim Fargo.

"You're right, Kim," answered Jim. "She hates this petty-ante underhanded stuff. We'll have to keep our heads down, so she doesn't throw us in jail." That was good for a nervous laugh, but they all had seen the wrath of Judge Francis in action and knew that they would have to tread lightly in her court the next day.

+++++++

"All rise."

"Here we go," whispered Russ.

"Just stay low," answered Carl. Maybe we won't get any on us.

"Is everybody here?"

"Yes, your Honor," answered the attorneys.

Indeed, everyone was there. Rulon, Donna, and Holly sat at their respective tables with their attorneys. Governor Phillips sat in the first row of the gallery flanked by his real estate partners. Jim Farmer was there and so were Bill Debers, Rulon's real estate agent, and Frankie. Councilman Elias Fraiser sat quietly slumped down at the end of the last row trying to be invisible.

"Alright, let's hear from Governor Phillips first. Welcome Governor. Please come to sit in the witness chair so we can all hear what you have to say." The Governor made his way to the front of the court. Once he was seated and sworn in, the judge asked, "Governor; could you tell us what you know about the real estate dealings in Cohassett Beach as it relates to this case?"

"Yes, your Honor. Rulon Drego is not an honest man..." and he proceeded to tell the court the same story he had related to Russ and Carl about his dealings with Rulon ending with…"I would not trust that S.O.B. as far as I could throw him."

"Err…thank you Governor." The Judge dismissed him, and he ambled out of the court room all the while glaring at Rulon.

"I think we can dismiss the Governor's partners as well," stated Judge Francis. "Let's hear from Donna Reis." Donna made her way to the witness chair and was sworn in by the clerk. The governor's entourage made their way out of the courtroom showing relief. "Ms. Reis, what do you have to say?

"I was misled. I believed that Rulon was going to help me acquire or give us the land for the Cohassett Beach Carousel. He enticed me to bed with that promise and then he reneged."

"Did you get your organization to work against the condo/marina project mentioned by the Governor?" the Judge asked.

"Yes, I did. Led on by Drego's false promises and all the while believing I was saving the community center. He never cared about the community center at all. All he cared about was acquiring land for his businesses and parking for his customers."

"Did Mr. Drego physically abuse you at any time?"

"No, your Honor."

"You gave yourself to him willingly?"

"Yes, your Honor, but he had made promises."

"Thank you, Ms. Reis. You are dismissed for now. Go back to the table."

"Ms. Richards." Holly promised to tell the truth and took her place on the witness chair. "Did Mr. Drego take any action personally against you or the café?"

"If you're asking did he personally send me into bankruptcy, no. But he worked to ruin my business so he could get his hands on the land. He sent that biker gang to bust up the place and set that fire in the dumpster."

"Those are serious charges, Ms. Richards."

"I know, your Honor, but he did it."

"Enough for now, Ms. Richards. Return to the table."

"Mr. Frank Fusco, please come forward."

Russ had to admit that Frankie cleaned up rather well. He had looked good at his trial when he had been convicted of transporting drugs. He looked as good today as he was sworn in with a fresh haircut and a smooth shave, except for the thin moustache.

"Mr. Fusco, I believe we are acquainted. You have been in my court before and are presently on parole."

"Yes, your Honor."

"Mr. Fusco did you aid or set the fire in the dumpster at the Cohassett Beach Café and did you arrange for your, ahem, group to have dinner there resulting in a melee that left the place in shambles?"

"Your Honor, we just went there..."

"Mr. Fusco...just answer the question."

"Yes, Ma'am. We took the actions you mentioned."

"Who asked you to take those actions?

"It was just…"

"Frankie…"

"Mr. Drego," Frankie said without looking up.

"Thank you, Mr. Fusco. You're dismissed. See the clerk for an appointment with my office before you depart the building. We need to settle the matter of your parole violations."

"Yes, your Honor."

Throughout the testimony, Rulon had sat quietly in his chair. With each witness, he seemed to shrink in size to the point that he was now hardly visible from the gallery.

"Mr. Drego, do you dispute any of these facts as presented here today?" Judge Francis asked looking directly at Rulon with very cold eyes.

"It was just business, your Honor."

"Very well. We will conduct *business* in my chambers at eleven tomorrow. Everyone is invited back; don't be late. That's all for today." Judge Francis concluded banging her gavel.

+++++++

"Governor Phillips," Judge Francis began precisely at eleven the following day, "Do you feel that you deserve anything out this whole affair."

"No, your Honor. No matter what happened, the Army Corp of Engineers killed my project and my group found another complex to develop. We are satisfied."

"Thank you, Governor. Thank you for your time." Governor Phillips made his way from the crowded chambers of the Judge and softly closed the door behind him.

"Mr. Fusco; having violated the terms of your parole, you are remanded to the custody of the sheriffs. They are waiting outside to escort you back to serve the rest of your sentence. You will meet the rest of your cohorts there." Frankie left in handcuffs in the company of two burly sheriffs.

"Ms. Richards; what would make you whole in all of this?"

"You Honor, I just want out of the restaurant business. I'm tired of the whole mess. If I could just break even, I would be happy."

Holly told the Judge what she originally paid for the café. The judge looked at Rulon.

"Mr. Drego, would you be willing to pay that amount for the property?"

"Yes, your Honor. That would be a fair price for the café and land."

"Then good. Are you willing to enter into an agreement with Ms. Richards stating as much?"

"Yes, your Honor.

"Good. Ms. Richards, please stay for a few moments." Ms. Reis, You have been deceitful as well. Your motivation was admirable, but you have betrayed your organization. Are you willing to resign as president of the Carousel Foundation?"

"Oh, your Honor. I have worked so hard and we are so close."

"But you lack one thing, don't you?"

"Yes, ma'am. We do not have land to put the carousel on."

"No, you don't, but to make this whole thing go away, Mr. Drego might be willing to donate the original site if you resign, won't you Mr. Drego. After all...you promised." Judge Francis smiled at Rulon until he answered.

Seeing no way out and feeling that he might risk his liquor license for Ellie's Pier, he looked at the judge and meekly answered, "Yes, your Honor."

"Good. Now there is the matter of these charges. You were a bad boy too Mr. Drego and I would think that the prosecutor would be looking to file new charges in the light of the recent testimony we have heard here. Do you think you might drop your charges against Ms. Reis and Ms. Richards with your wounds healing so nicely and we might be able to conclude these proceedings today?"

Rulon, to his credit, had caught on that the judge had him in a box. "Yes, Your Honor."

"Good. This mater is concluded, my thanks to the attorneys and the detectives. I love it when a plan comes together."

Chapter 25: Who Says You Can't Go Home?

"How was your barbeque Saturday at your in-laws?" asked Russ.

"Oh, Big Ern's welcome home bash was all you could imagine. All of his friends were there, and he acted like nothing happened. He lost some hair while he was in prison, but he looks good."

"I don't doubt it. His brother, Dino, might be in charge, but I'm sure it's still Big Ern's dealership."

"Oh, to be sure. He's back in the saddle again. Joelle was happy to see her Dad though. Big Ern and Dino tried to double-team me to get me to work at the dealership. They just won't ever take no for an answer."

"They just want you in the family business, but I'm glad you're smarter than that. Did Joelle behave herself or did she take you down to the pool house again?"

"A gentleman never tells." But his smile told it all. "How about the four of us go down to Ellie's Pier Friday night? I hear the restaurant is really good," Carl asked trying to change the subject.

"I'm sure Rulon would be happy to see us," Russ said with a smile.

"In the end, he really did get what he wanted. The doughboy shop, a new restaurant, and all the parking he ever could wish for," said Carl.

"And a carousel to draw even more crowds in," added Russ.

"That and a totally new beach, seawall, and beach parking. He is still the king of Cohassett Beach. Maybe the King will buy us a drink," suggested Carl.

"I wouldn't go that far."

+++++++

The ladies dressed to the nines for dinner. Carl and Joelle picked up Russ and Sophia and drove to the restaurant. Russ opened the door for Sophia to get out of the rear door of Carl's SUV and he admired the long slender legs that Sophia allowed him to see as she exited the car.

"Like what you see big boy," she asked giving him a wink.

"Always...and I'd like to see more," Russ quipped.

"Play your cards right and buy me a nice dinner and you just might get your wish," Sophia whispered as she brushed against him.

"Giddy up," Russ said taking her hand.

The couple had parked across the street from Ellie's Pier next to the new Carousel installation. They could hear the music from the ancient mechanism echoing down toward the beach.

"The carousel adds a lot of gaiety to the atmosphere. Don't you think?" Joelle asked.

"I love it," answered Sophia. "It puts me in a festive mood."

"They crossed the street and entered Ellie's Pier Restaurant. There was a bit of a line and they were told that it would be twenty or thirty minutes before they would be seated.

They spotted two seats at the bar. The girls took the seats and the boys stood behind them. They ordered drinks.

"Is this your first time here," Sophia asked Joelle.

"It is. The place is beautiful," Joelle said looking around at the bar and dining room. "The bar woodwork is magnificent and the view out across the bay is fabulous."

"I'm told that the food is terrific. I asked for a table at the windows. I hope we get that to see the boats coming in. That really would be nice."

The bartender brought the drinks and Russ held out money to pay. An arm came in from behind him and covered his hand and the bills.

"That's alright, Angelo. These people are my guests. The drinks are on the house," said Rulon.

"Thank you very much, Mr. Drego," said Russ. "You remember my partner Carl Resendez. This is his wife Joelle, and this is Sophia whom you have met."

Rulon was gracious in his greeting the women and offered to seat them immediately.

"Thank you, Mr. Drego, but our tables will be ready in just a few minutes we are told," said Carl.

"As you wish; still I'll check for you. I hope we can be friends. Cohassett Beach is a friendly place and we will all be here for a long time. Enjoy your dinner. I'll check on your table."

"He seems like a friendly guy," Sophia said when Rulon was out of earshot.

"He may seem friendly," said Carl, "But be careful when you shake hands, you might find a couple of fingers gone." At that their buzzer on the bar went off with flashing lights indicating that their table was ready.

The couples made their way back to the receptionist's podium and were immediately led to a table by the window. The window was open slightly and the warm, evening breeze made its way into the restaurant lending a salty aroma to the air. The dining room was equally elegant with fancy lighting and ceiling fans. The intricate wood patterns on the ceiling and color were interesting.

They ordered dinner and another round of drinks. They were thoroughly enjoying themselves when the girls excused themselves to go to the powder room. Once they were gone, Russ said to Carl, "You sure you don't want to go with Joelle to christen the new restaurant?"

"Some other time," Carl smiled. "Hey, Rulon bought us a round. Maybe he's trying to make amends?"

"He's got a lot to make up for, but I don't think he's turning over a new leaf just yet. Judge Francis had his gonads in a vice, so he gave in, but he didn't seem to like it all that much."

"No, he didn't. I guess it's best to keep him at arm's length."

"You bet. Welcome back ladies. You all look fresh as daisies. What's next for this evening?" asked Russ as he and Carl held the girls' chairs as they sat.

"Do you think we were planning in there?" asked Sophia.

"Plotting would be more like it," said Carl. "So, what are we doing after this?"

"We thought it would be nice to go and ride the Carousel," said Joelle.

"Well, I guess no trip to the new Cohassett Beach would be complete without a ride on the Carousel," said Carl. "Too bad they don't have a 'Tunnel of Love' anymore. That could be interesting."

"Okay, you two. Try to hold it together through dinner and a Carousel ride. Oh, here is our dinner. It looks scrumptious."

And indeed, the food was as good as advertised. Rulon had done it up right with a fine chef and a beautiful restaurant. Everyone wished him well as they left and hoped for better times at the beach.

After dinner, the two couples went for a stroll down to the beach and onto the boardwalk. They were walking hand in hand with Russ and Sophia in front.

"This walk is helping my dinner settle before we go on the Carousel," said Russ.

Carl let out a low belch, "Yeah, me too."

The group laughed and continued their walk. On the way up the hill they had to walk out in the street because the sidewalk was taken up by the lines at Ellie's Doughboy Shop. Once by that, they went back on to the sidewalk and were passing across the street from Ellie's Pier and the apartment building when Russ stopped in mid-stride. He was staring up at the top of the apartment building.

"Would you look at that," he said.

"What said Carl?" they were all looking in the same direction and trying to see what Russ was seeing.

"Look at the dark letters bleeding through the white paint on the building. It says DODG'EM. It's where the old dodgem cars used to be in the era of the amusement park before the storms. That building is the only original building left other than the doughboy shop. The rest were wiped out by hurricanes."

They continued their walk-in silence. There was an elderly couple walking in front of them and they separated to go around them. Russ turned back as they passed, "Ed...Dot...is that you?"

"Russell," Dot said. "It is so good to see you."

"Sophia, this is Dot and Ed. I used to live in their apartment in North Providence before I moved to Cohassett Beach. And this is my partner on the police force, Carl and his wife, Joelle." Greetings were exchanged all around.

"We read about you in the paper all the time. It seems you are doing well." Dot said.

Yes. Yes, I am. I graduated law school last year and passed the bar," said Russ.

"I remember you going to school nights when you lived in the apartment., Congratulations" said Ed.

"Did you come down here to go to the new restaurant?" asked Joelle.

"No. We went to the doughboy shop like we used to do in the old days when we used to bring our children here," said Dot.

"This place was really something before the hurricanes," said Ed. "I used to come here with my friends on the trolley back in the '30's. It was a great adventure for us."

"Are you headed for the Carousel?" asked Dot.

"Yes, we are," answered Sophia. "We have not ridden the new Carousel yet. Have you?"

"No, this will be our first time," said Dot.

They reached the Carousel building and were overwhelmed by the calliope of music. They bought tickets and boarded the ride. The couples chose their horses on the outside and Dot and Ed took a circus wagon.

The carvings were beautiful. The horses and wagons had great detail in the wood and the painting brought back the wonder of the old carousel rides that used to be in many small amusement parks all over the country. Once the ride got up to speed, a man climbed the platform and dumped metal rings into the box. He then swung the arm out so that those on the outside could snatch a ring with their finger as they passed.

As it always had been, most of the rings were steel, but a few of them were brass. Brass rings could be cashed in for a free-ride ticket. Steel rings were tossed into the booth at the clown's face, with a hole where the clown's nose should be, acting as a target.

Russ snatched a brass ring on his first try. The others kept getting steel rings and tossing them at the clown until Joelle got a brass ring toward the end. She let out a whoop when she saw it.

They all got off the ride giggling and laughing. For some reason, a carousel brings happiness to all that ride it. It may be the music, or it may be the motion. Maybe it is all the colors, but it happens every time.

Dot and Ed were standing off to the side. "Did you enjoy your ride?" Russ asked.

"Oh, it was marvelous. It was just like years ago," said Dot.

"Here, take one more spin," and Russ handed Ed the two brass rings.

As Russ, Sophia, Carl, and Joelle were walking away, they could see Dot and Ed whirling around on the carousel in their circus carriage, laughing and acting like they were teenagers again.

About the Author

DJ Charpentier is a retired educator. Mr. Charpentier also served over twenty years in the Rhode Island Air National Guard. *As Luck Would Have It (First Edition)* was his first full length manuscript in which he shared his experiences concerning saving for and coping with retirement. That writing has twice been updated. *As Luck Would Have It* titled *5 Years Later* updates the original writing and Retire Well! Is the latest...a ten-year update.

Bethany Blues, Ocean City Blues, and Key West Blues which chronicles the adventures of Reggie Slater, Joe, and Sandra and all their friends. *Beach Blues, Marginal Blues, and Carousel Blues* are part of the Russ Deever series along with the recently published *Return to Bethany Beach*. All are available at Amazon.com in both e-book and print format. Mr. Charpentier lives is Rhode Island and travels extensively with his wife in their motor home throughout the United States.

Now available by request is DJ Charpentier's first album *"In My Dreams"* produced by Dave Furlong at *The Music Room* in Richmond, Rhode Island.

From the author:

I enjoy getting mail from readers and attempt to answer all email. Please, do not send snail mail. With all the traveling we do, there is no way I can answer those promptly. If you do want an answer, please send email to DPCharp@gmail.com .

Writing is something I find extremely enjoyable and wish I had started writing fiction years ago. I enjoy reading because a well-crafted story transports you to a place and immerses you in another world. Writing does the same except you can craft that world and manipulate the characters to fit what you wish to happen. It is a lot of work, but the rewards greatly outweigh the pain.

DJ Charpentier

Acknowledgement

I want to make mention and special thank you again to my wife Pat and daughters Jess and Lori. They have helped my effort to produce this book in several ways, some I may not fully understand or ever know; my thanks to you for having the patience to put up with me.

And thanks so much once again to the great song writers and bands that once again supplied some of the inspirational lyrics and song titles, I have used in the chapter titles in the manuscript. Their music continues to be an inspiration for writing and provides great enjoyment in my life.

Made in the USA
Monee, IL
20 May 2021